FAMOUS PEOPLE

FAMOUS PEOPLE

A NOVEL

JUSTIN KURITZKES

HENRY HOLT AND COMPANY   NEW YORK

Henry Holt and Company
Publishers since 1866
175 Fifth Avenue
New York, New York 10010
www.henryholt.com

Henry Holt® and 🅜® are registered trademarks of
Macmillan Publishing Group, LLC.

Library of Congress Cataloging-in-Publication Data

Names: Kuritzkes, Justin, author.
Title: Famous people : a novel / Justin Kuritzkes.
Description: First edition. | New York : Henry Holt and Company, 2019.
Identifiers: LCCN 2018038351 | ISBN 9781250309020 (hardcover)
Subjects: LCSH: Celebrities—Fiction. | Self-perception—Fiction.
Classification: LCC PS3611.U73228 F36 2019 | DDC 813/.6—dc23
LC record available at https://lccn.loc.gov/2018038351

Our books may be purchased in bulk for promotional, educational, or business
use. Please contact your local bookseller or the Macmillan Corporate and
Premium Sales Department at (800) 221-7945, extension 5442, or by e-mail
at MacmillanSpecialMarkets@macmillan.com.

This is a work of fiction. All of the characters, organizations, and events
portrayed in this novel are either products of the author's imagination or
are used fictitiously.

First Edition 2019

Printed in the United States of America

1   3   5   7   9   10   8   6   4   2

For Celine

FAMOUS PEOPLE

I been famous since I was twelve. Made a vid of me singing the national anthem that got like, ten million views in its first week because I was doing some crazy shit with my voice. I used to be able to hit high notes—like the kind that girls can—before my voice dropped. Now my voice is still tight—I'm not gonna be falsely modest or whatever—but it used to be like, ACTUALLY dope. You know what I mean?

The thing about being famous for so long is that like, you never really hang with any normal people anymore, because it's just weird for everybody. But at the same time, you're *more* connected to normal people than even most normal people are, because you're one of the very few people on Earth who actually looks at them. Most normal people just look at my life—or they look at the lives of other people like me—and they just spend all their time thinking about how dope it would be, like, how absolutely next-level it would be to be me, and so they're never really looking at themselves. But then they all show up at my concert—they're all gathered there, like thousands of them—and it's like they're all just lined up for me to examine them. Sometimes it's like five nights a week that I'm just staring into this massive crowd of normal people—and I'm like: Guys . . . I *get* you. I see what you're all about.

Here's my daily grind:

I get up, I go to the studio, I turn out some tracks, I go to the gym, I go take my singing lessons, I go take my guitar lessons—I can play all the chords, but I want to get GOOD—I take meetings. I listen to shit.

So much time is spent just listening to shit.

Sometimes I'm on the road. That's all right. It's never as fun as you think it's going to be. Sometimes it's mind-blowingly dope, but then other times you just want to be like: Okay, fuck Tennessee. But you *can't* just say fuck Tennessee because then Tennessee is gonna be like: Fuck *this* kid. This kid is a stuck-up little bitch who doesn't care about our time. And I *do* care about people's time. It means so much to me that people buy tickets to my shows—they wait in lines for hours, for days even, just to hear the songs they've already heard a million times on the radio. Once I've committed to something, I NEVER, I repeat: NEVER back out, because in a way, it's like . . . that's the least I can do, you know? People are dying all over the world. People are getting blown up every day. The environment is fucking breaking down. Shit is tough out there. People's lives are tough. And like, what? I'm gonna miss a whole fucking concert because I don't feel like it? Nah.

A while back, I had this realization. I just started thinking, like: I could do more. I could still be grateful for my success and all, and like, I could still wake up every day and try to kill it, but I could do so much more. And that's when I decided to write this book.

The publishers had been reaching out to me for a while. It's no secret that any book with my name on it is gonna move a lot of units. That's not me being arrogant or whatever, that's just a fact. They had been on me to work with a ghostwriter and churn out a memoir, and a little while back, I finally said to myself: You know what? It's time. I'm ready to tell my story. I'm ready to put into words what I've learned about life. No ghostwriters, though— this shit's gonna be straight from the source.

And I don't mean to say that I have anything to teach anybody—really I don't. If anything, this book is about the people who taught *me*, the people who made me who I am.

I guess it's more like this: I've led a very singular life— I've had a very particular kind of experience on this Earth—and I think people might be interested to hear what the world looks like through my eyes, to step into my mind.

Why I really decided to write this book now is like, the world seems to be spinning out of control, you know? People are so mad at each other. People are taking life so seriously. People are losing hope. And I think, honestly, it's because people are so rooted in their own particular spot in the universe.

But something happens to you when you're touring all around the world all the time. Something happens to you when you visit some country you've never heard of and you see your face on the side of a bus being used to sell some soda that you didn't even know existed, and you call up your people and you're like: Yo, did we agree to this? And they tell you: Yes, it was part of an overall deal with East Asia.

Something happens: You realize how fucking tiny you are.

Honestly, that's what amazes me the most with a lot of the people I meet: They think they're so big. They think, ultimately, that the universe revolves around them. And I'm beginning to think that it's only when you live a life like mine—it's only when you're in a position where you don't even really own yourself, when you can't even really say that you're a citizen of any particular country—that you realize that we're all just tiny pieces of cosmic dust floating through the void until we disappear forever and we're never heard from again.

I'm not saying that *all* famous people understand this. Definitely some of the worst, like, most horrible people I've ever met are famous people. But most of those people are only *kind of* famous, or even *pretty* famous, because for them, like, they're still a part of the normal people world—they've still got a normal people mentality—but they just feel like they're at the *top* of that world, you know? They feel like they're the KINGS and QUEENS of the normal people world. And those people are the fucking worst. But the *truly* famous people, the like, insanely famous people—the kinds of people who have their faces on buses in countries they've never heard of—most of those people are pretty chill. I've honestly never met a single one of those people who I didn't immediately get along with. And I think it's because we all have something in common. We all speak the same language. We all understand that in a hundred years, even if our records are still available to stream online, even if our merchandise is still lining the shelves, even if our autobiographies are still bestsellers, we're all gonna be *gone*, you know? And when you're gone, you're GONE. It doesn't matter what it says on your Wikipedia page, or if you even *have* a Wikipedia page in the first place. Life's funny like that. LOL.

But let's backtrack a bit. I want you to get the full picture. I want you to know where I'm coming from—I want you to feel like you have a firm foundation for understanding the person who's writing these words—so let's go to the beginning.

This is kind of weird for me to say, but it's actually kind of hard for me to remember anything that happened in my life before I was famous. I guess it's hard for most people to remember the stuff that was happening to them before they were twelve, but for me it's especially hard because the video blowing up and all of that shit happening marks a very clear line in my life. The life that I'm living now is still in some ways the same life that was birthed the day I uploaded that thing, and so the life before that feels like . . . another time. A different movie.

I was born in St. James Hospital in St. James, Minnesota. My mom was a dental assistant. My dad was a sound engineer at the local radio station: KLRX. I say "was" with my mom because she's not a dental assistant anymore—I gave her a BUNCH of money so she's good—and I say "was" with my dad because he's dead.

Actually, I don't really want to get into this right now, but my dad killed himself. He fucked himself up. Shotgun to the face. Most of you probably already knew that. And that was AFTER I was famous, so I remember that day. I mean, I wasn't there—we had been estranged for a minute—but I remember finding out about it. I didn't even get a phone call from the police or anything. I was on an airplane when it happened, and so when I got off at the gate, immediately this paparazzi motherfucker came up to me and he was like: Yo, how do you feel about your dad? And I was like: Listen, I've told you people everything I have to say about my dad already. Stop asking me about him. And he was like: But how do you feel about what happened today? And I was like: What are you talking about? And he—I mean, there were a bunch of other paparazzi people there too, you know, and all of them just went like, suddenly silent. Like, all of them just kind of looked at each other and they were like: This is fucked up. Like, even the paparazzi guys were like: This isn't how he should find out. But I could tell that something was up—I mean, I'd never seen a paparazzi act like this before—and so I was like: What the fuck are you talking about? And the paparazzi guy was like, really nervous to say it—like, he felt really bad—but none of the other paparazzi people were gonna do it for him—he knew that it was his duty at this point—and so he just stammered out: He . . . he killed himself. Your dad's dead. And the way he said it, like, I just knew it was true. I just saw the whole thing in my

JUSTIN KURITZKES

mind. And the paparazzi people were all, like, watching me come to realize it, and their cameras were rolling on me, and nobody was saying anything, and then I just fucking booked it. My security guards were pushing people out of the way, going full linebacker mode. And I've watched the videos of me doing this a couple of times. There's a few different videos online that have been uploaded because, you know, there were a few different paparazzi guys there. And some of them are sort of close up on my face hearing the news and some of them are wider, giving a view of the whole thing, and there's this one video that's got almost as many views as that first video of me singing the national anthem, and that's the one I watch sometimes.

But I grew up in just a regular town. I was just like, a regular kid. I started singing in church. We were part of this small church, this like, really tiny local church, and we had this choir director, and he wasn't black, but he had us only singing black songs. He would always say: Black church is what *all* church should aspire to be. And so he had us singing like, traditional black music, you know, and we really went for it. None of us were black, but we were really committed. I would do all the solos because I had like, this next-level voice, and I remember the choir director taking me aside one day and saying: Boy, you got the SPIRIT in you! And I guess that's when I first realized that I had something special. I mean, I've never talked to God—some people have. Some people in the choir said they did—but when I'm singing, it's like sometimes I can *feel* him, you know?

So I sang in the church choir, and my parents would

come and watch me, and they were really proud—the whole town was—and that was pretty tight, to be honest. My mom would come to our Friday Night Praises after a long week of working with the dentist, and my singing would just put the color back into her face. And my dad— he immediately understood the potential of what I had. He was like, immediately saying that I couldn't just save it for the church. He had a context for understanding that, you know, because he worked at the radio. Whenever a big pop star would come through town to play a concert in Minneapolis, they would go on the morning show to promote it, and my dad would get to like, meet all these people and their managers and whatever, and so he was like: My son could be one of these people. My son could be killing it one day if he plays his cards right.

And so he started talking like he was my manager. Before any of this shit even happened, you know, before anyone knew who I was, my dad was like: We're gonna build this thing together. And I was cool with that. I mean, I was twelve, you know, so he was just like, my daddy to me—I would've been cool with anything he wanted—but I think even at that age, I realized that we might make good business partners. We both had that *fire* in us, you know? We both just wanted to crush it.

And there was definitely a time before I was born, or like, early in my childhood, when my dad wanted to crush it himself. No question about it. He was in a band before he started working at the radio, and he'd still play in some bands every once in a while, and for a second it looked like his grunge band was gonna have a moment, but by the time that was happening, the grunge thing was already kinda done, and so my dad's band just got left behind, and he transferred all his hopes of killing it onto me. And I was fine with that, honestly. I mean, I liked that he was so invested.

He started having me make these recordings: just like, little CDs of me singing whatever was number one on the radio that week. He'd get the instrumental tracks from the station—'cause sometimes they'd play the instrumentals from a song while they were doing an advertisement or an intro or something—and he'd bring me to the station after hours, and we'd mix a version where I was singing it instead of whoever the artist was, and then when a big-time artist or a big-time manager came into town, he'd try to pass off the CDs to them at the radio station and be like: Yo man, you gotta listen to my boy. You gotta listen to my son.

And those tracks are fucking DOPE. I mean, seriously, I still listen to them sometimes. They're like, actually kinda next-level. I talked to my manager—my new manager—about maybe releasing them as a covers album, you know, just like, this crazy thing that no one knows exists that I made before I was famous, but she told me it's gonna get complicated with the rights and the licensing and whatever, and so I've put it on the back burner for now.

But yeah, we were trying to break in, making these recordings, getting better and better at it, and then one day my dad had this realization:

People have to SEE you. It's not enough that they hear your voice. They've gotta see that this voice is coming from this adorable, totally normal little kid. Your voice sounds like money, it sounds like this beautiful, polished, Madison Square Garden thing, but they've gotta see your shitty little room and your normal fucking posters and your GI Joes and all that shit or else they won't have the right context. They've gotta feel like they're discovering you.

And so we recorded this video. We like, set-dressed my room to make it look even more normal than it was, and we tried on a bunch of these different outfits in the mirror, and if something looked too good or too hip, we'd take it off and try something new. And when we were thinking about which song to sing, at first we tried all these hits that were on the radio around that time—you know, the same kind of shit we had been recording on the CDs—but then my dad was like: Hold on. And I was like: What? And he was like: It's the Fourth of July soon. And I was like: Shit. And he was like: You gotta sing the national anthem. And I was like: Genius.

And I killed it. First take. I'm not trying to brag or whatever, but if you've seen the video, you know. I just totally fucking killed it. At the end, I had this moment of inspiration—it was just like, this sudden epiphany. All of a sudden, I said: Happy Fourth of July, everybody. Stay safe. And I threw up a peace sign. And my dad let the camera roll for a second—we were just using the camera that was on the computer—and then he stopped it and he looked at me, and he was like: That's it. And I was like: You think? And he was like: Yeah.

And he was right.

• • •

Okay, so I know everyone who picks up this book is gonna be like: Where's the part where he talks about Mandy? What's he gonna say about Mandy? So let's just get it out of the way.

Mandy and I got together pretty much when I first moved out to L.A. So I was like . . . fourteen at that point. LOL. My dad didn't want to move us out until we already had a hit on the radio, so we recorded the whole record in Minnesota, put it out while we were still there, and then finally rolled into town on this wave of insane exposure with "Be My Baby" and "Don't Look Back." It was weird— my dad had been waiting his whole life for something like this to happen, but now that it was happening, he was being so methodical about it, so patient. He was like, enveloped in this force field of cool. None of it stressed him out at all. It was really beautiful to watch.

Mandy and I met at this party the label threw called the Up and Comers Ball. Basically, it was a big plot to get us to bone. The party was this private thing at the head of the label's place in Malibu, and the whole idea was for the young people on the label to meet each other and see if they wanted to collaborate, but Mandy's agent told her later that it was all about us. Everyone had sort of come to the conclusion that it would give each of us a boost, and they knew they couldn't just tell us to start dating each other, so they threw this big party instead. And it was weird, because, like, looking back on it, at the time it really felt like we were having this genuine chance encounter with each other, but actually, the whole night there were people pushing us together. Like, people kept mentioning her to me—and me to her obviously—and I actually think that people were, like, moving around the room so that we could be alone together. Like, if we were in a circle with a few other people, everyone would super-subtly but also really efficiently excuse themselves to go do something else, and so we'd find ourselves talking just the two of us.

And it worked. I mean, how could it not? Mandy's like, beautiful, and at that point, I had the number one song on the radio, and so the math just added up. Plus, I think we actually really liked each other. Mandy was from a small town too—she grew up in Mobile, Arizona—and so both of us were looking around at all this L.A. shit being like: What fucking planet are we on? LOL.

And for the record, just 'cause I know there's some people who still don't believe us: Yeah, we lost our V-cards to each other. I took Mandy's, and she took mine, and I'll always remember her for that. I came in ten seconds flat. Seriously. My poor little guy didn't stand a chance. I was talking all this big game beforehand like: Yo, I bet I'll last at least a couple minutes, maybe half an hour. But then the second my dick hit pussy, it was just like: NOPE! HERE WE GO!

Mandy's pussy is like . . . how can I describe Mandy's pussy . . .

YO! I'm just kidding! I'm not gonna divulge that kind of shit to you guys! Are you serious? Mandy's gonna be someone's mom someday! If you want to read about that kind of shit, go to the message boards. Go read the tabloids. Go plug yourself into whatever misinformation machine you've got waiting for you in your browser. That shit's gotten out of hand. I was hooking up with this one girl after a show, and before I took my pants off she was like: So is it true? And I was like: Is what true? And she was like: Do you really have all the lyrics to your songs tattooed on your dick? And I was just like: How is that even possible? Even if I included the balls, how small would they have to write? I'm not saying I'm lacking in hardware, but like: Seriously? I'm gonna spend *that* much time with some tattoo artist, letting him hold my thing in his hand while he inserts a needle into it again and again? Are you kidding me?

Actually, that reminds me: I've asked the publisher to let me include an appendix at the back of the book where I'll have a little diagram of all the tattoos on my body and explain the significance of each one. I'm kind of sick of all these articles online that I've seen that try to catalog them, because like, first of all, they always miss a few, and second, like, they come up with all these totally insane, absolutely ridiculous explanations for what they represent, and so I'd rather just give you the official tally. Obviously, it'll only be valid up to the date of publication, since I can pretty much guarantee that I'll be getting fresh ink up until the day I die, but maybe if they print a second edition of the book, I'll update it. Who knows?

But yo! My first tattoo was with Mandy. We went and got them together. We were like, walking around on the beach one day in Santa Monica, and we had some popcorn or whatever—you know, we bought it from one of the vendors on the pier—and this bird just swooped down and jacked the popcorn right out of my hand. Mandy and I were laughing about it, and we were like: Yo, that was crazy! What kind of bird was that? And we asked this old, like, surfer dude on the beach, like: Hey, do you know what these birds are around here? And we like, pointed at one, and he was like: Seriously? And we were like: Yeah, what are these called? And he was like: That's a seagull, man. What the fuck? And Mandy and I immediately started cracking up because we had obviously seen them in movies and like, seen drawings of them when we were in kindergarten and seen them around L.A., but neither of us had actually ever put the pieces together and been like: oh, *that's* what a seagull looks like.

And this was right after we had lost our virginities to each other, so we just felt like it was the two of us forever. You know how that feels? When it's first love? You're just like: Whoa, okay, this is obviously the only person I'm ever gonna be with. Like, obviously, I can't ever feel this way about *someone else*. And so later that night, we passed by a tattoo parlor, and we were just like: Absolutely. Let's do it.

You're supposed to have, like, a written permission slip from your mom or whatever when you're that young, but the guys at the tattoo parlor had seen us both on TV, and so they thought it would be tight to give us both our first ink. And so we each got a little seagull right above our hearts. Just a simple little guy. It's a really sweet first tattoo when I think about it. I'm glad it wasn't something stupid like her name or a rose or whatever. It's just this little seagull. I love that thing. Every time I look at it in the mirror after I get out of the shower, I think of Mandy. It's crazy how in love we were then.

But life is this ever-changing thing, you know? You have to accept that. Everything is just a phase that's passing through us. And we're all just phases that are passing through the world. Things aren't supposed to last forever. Not even tattoos.

Things started going sour with my dad around the time I was releasing my second album. The first album was like, obviously this major hit, and now everybody was just waiting to see what the second album was gonna be, and my dad had already sort of mapped it out—he already had a plan for it even before we dropped the first one—and he hadn't really let me in on the plan, because he was just like: Focus on the shows. Focus on the interviews. Focus on the battle at hand. But then when it came time to start recording, he showed me what he was thinking and I was just like . . . Nah. That's not it.

I mean, I could see what he was going for. The first album had been like, all about me being a kid, you know? It was this very pure, sort of really catchy and hot, but like, very innocent thing. The big single, "Be My Baby," was all about me having a crush on this girl and like, writing her notes in class, but she never got the notes because somehow they'd always get intercepted by other kids along the way, and it was totally cute. Like, it wasn't SO childish that adults couldn't sing it or play it in the background while they were working out, but it wasn't so adult that it felt like I was faking something. But now I was a *teenager.* Now I was living in a totally different reality. Now I was in L.A., and like . . . I wasn't a *virgin* anymore, you know what I'm saying?

Think back to when you were fifteen, and try to

remember how badly you just wanted to fuck somebody. Like, when you were fifteen, were you ever thinking about anything OTHER than fucking somebody? And it was probably really hard to make that happen, right? Because, like, *what are you gonna do?* I mean, sure, tons of kids these days are bumping by fifteen—twelve even—but I'm just saying, like, when you're that age, all you want to do is just be an adult already, but you can't, because you're living with your parents, and you don't have any of your own money, and you can't go to bars or go to clubs or anything, and you're just like, this horny, helpless, powerless little person.

But I was *actually* doing all those things that fifteen-year-olds dream about, and I was doing them *when I was fifteen*. I mean, I have a theory about this, and I think the problem with so many people—well, I guess I should just say men, because I don't know what it's like to be a woman—but the problem with so many men is that they have to wait until they're like, thirty to live the life they dreamed of when they were fifteen. And that's if they're LUCKY, you know? But here I was, like, ACTUALLY fifteen years old, and I was living the fucking dream! I was partying, and going out to bars, and making my own millions, and fucking girls—Mandy and I were on a break at that point because she thought maybe she was a lesbian—and so I felt like an adult. For all intents and purposes, I WAS an adult. I mean, I was filing taxes—not by myself, but like, the taxes had my name on them—and so I was seeing the world and seeing myself way differently than I did when I was singing in the choir.

And I mean, I should also say, like, my voice was

changing at this point, you know? I just literally couldn't sing the kinds of songs that I sang on the first album. Even if I had wanted to, I just physically couldn't hit those notes anymore.

But my dad had written me all these songs for the second album, and like, they were about *teenage* shit, you know? Like, they were about NORMAL teenage shit. Honestly, looking back on it, I'm pretty sure that a lot of the songs were about stuff that like, my *dad* was feeling and going through when *he* was a teenager. And sure, some of those things were the same things I was going through, but for the most part, our lives were just completely different, and I couldn't really find much to connect with.

And, you know, when you're famous—when you're like, at the top of the charts and you're in L.A. and you've got the kind of fan base that I have—you meet people. You meet tons of people. And you'd be surprised by the kinds of people who want to work with you. I mean, even people who thought my first record was lame or whatever—you know, like, even people who thought I made music for kids—even they couldn't deny my numbers. No one can turn their nose up at the kind of units I was pushing. And so I found myself in this position where I could call up, like, dope musicians, like, really dope people who I really respected, and I could be like: Yo, you wanna get in the studio today? And more often than not, they'd be like: Yeah, let's go.

And so, without telling my dad—I mean, I wasn't trying to go behind his back or whatever. I was just doing my thing, being creative with whoever I wanted—I would go chill with all these guys making sick music around L.A. We'd smoke weed or go get a hamburger and then we'd usually get around to making some tracks, and you know, it was guys like Z Bunny and Trick Hatz and Deez Soundzz—just like, really dope, really forward-thinking, really crazy guys who had been in the game for a while. And it's not like I was even trying to put an album together—I just, like, after hanging with these guys every once in a while for a couple months, realized that I had a whole bunch of songs and that all of them were a lot more exciting to me than the stuff my dad and I had been working on.

And so one day, I was chilling with Deez Soundzz, and you know, he's kind of crazy, like he's kind of one of those guys who, when he gets that certain look in his eyes, you know he's about to say some insane shit, and like, we were chilling with these girls, and they knew I was fifteen, but whatever, they were down, and we were in the jacuzzi at Deez's place, and we were playing this track we had made for the girls on the speakers out there, and they were like, losing their minds over it. And, at some point, one of them was like: When is this coming out, Deez? And Deez just looked at me straight in the face, and he was like: Tonight, bitches. And I was like, immediately laughing and shit, like, I thought he was joking, but Deez was like: I'm serious, bro. Let's roll the dice. And I was feeling kind of like . . . I don't know, I was feeling like life was full of *possibility*, you know? I was feeling like life was so *ridiculous*. I was feeling like why be so precious about this second album? Who cared? I had so much to give the world, and like, not everything needs a strategy. Not everything needs a plan. Sometimes, you just gotta let inspiration take you—you just gotta make a bold, crazy move, and if people don't like it, fuck 'em. Move on.

And so Deez dropped it on his website that night—he just put it out there—and within an hour, it felt like the whole world had heard it. People were losing their shit. Deez and I didn't even sit there at the computer or anything waiting for the responses to roll in. We just went out and got some sushi. We ordered sake and beer, and we just sat back and watched our phones blow up. The girls we were with were like, cracking up every time one of our phones rang, and eventually, we both just turned them off, and Deez was like: Let's go perform this shit. And I was laughing, like: *Where*, Deez? And Deez was just like: Where you think, homie? Charizard.

And so without even announcing it or anything, we just rolled into Charizard and got ready to play. We walked in the door, and immediately, the staff knew what was up. They laid out a sound board for Deez, and they got him a laptop, and they got me a microphone and within, like, fifteen minutes, there was this insane crowd outside. I don't even know how all these people got there so fast, but it was this crazy mixture of Deez's fans and my fans, and I talked to the bouncer, and I was like: Yo, man, a lot of my fans are underage. Think you can give 'em a pass? And he was like: Yeah, bro, I got you. This song is tight. And so within half an hour, the house was packed. Deez and I were set up, and we didn't even sound check or anything, we were just riding on this, like, insane high. And we let it rip. I mean . . . we crushed it. I'm seriously not trying to brag or anything, but we just totally crushed it. It was legendary. A new era had begun.

Okay, so I want to tell you about someone.

One of the cool things about writing this book is that, like, I get to just talk about whatever I want whenever I want—I have all this space, and so I can just talk about all of the people who have had an impact on my life, who have left an impression—and so one person I definitely want to talk about is Oddvar, my biggest fan.

I know that sounds crazy—like, how can I know that he's my *biggest* fan?—but I'd honestly be *astounded* if there was anyone on the planet who cared more about me or my life than Oddvar. Oddvar's level of fandom is *off the fucking charts*. He's an EXPERT. He's a MASTER. And he's actually super-fucking-chill.

Being famous is crazy—that's true for so many reasons—but absolutely one of the craziest things about being famous—and like, this is one of those things that only the people who have experienced it can even begin to understand—is having fans. It's one thing to put shit out there and have people listen to it and like it or whatever or like, maybe play it at a party where they're all hanging or hear it on the radio and go crazy, but then there's this whole other thing, you know, where like, people are FANS of YOU. They've just decided that, like, YOU'RE the thing they're into, like, YOU'RE the thing they love most about life. And that's one hundred percent bizarre and insane every time you encounter it. You honestly never get used to it.

I was thinking about this the other day, because in L.A., they'll sometimes host conventions for sci-fi shit or fantasy shit, you know—like, they'll do it at the Convention Center downtown, and it'll be going on for a couple days—and I remember we were driving by the Convention Center one day on our way to this fashion show in Chinatown, and we saw this massive line of people with their tickets, all dressed up in their costumes waiting to get in. And you know, it was like, people were dressed as elves and wizards and battle dragons—it's not like they picked this shit up at the store: they MADE this shit—and I was just looking at all these people thinking: You guys LOVE this. Like, this is your FAVORITE thing. And I was just thinking about how crazy it is to love something that much—to devote such a big part of your life to being part of the world of something—and then it dawned on me, like: There are people who feel this way about ME. There are people who show up to meetings and symposiums and conventions and have like, full-on roundtable discussions about ME and my work. And I've honestly pretended for most of my life like that part of the world doesn't exist, but now that I'm writing this book and I'm thinking about who's actually gonna read it, it's like: Who ARE these people, you know? What are their lives like?

Honestly, I think part of the reason I've connected so much with Oddvar—like, part of the reason we've kept up a correspondence and become friends—is that he's totally not what I was expecting.

First of all, he's thirty-six years old—LOL—and second, he's this dude who lives in Norway—or well, not technically in Norway: He lives on this island called Spitsbergen in this region called Svalbard where like, there's this giant seed vault where they're keeping spare copies of seeds for basically every type of plant on Earth. Oddvar's job is to like, oversee the vault and to make sure all the seeds are being kept at the right temperature and to accept new seed deposits when they come in. I'm not kidding. That's what he does.

I forget exactly what he told me about the whole thing, but the way he described it, it's like: Basically, because this island is super-remote and it's super-cold there, they've stored all these seeds in the middle of this icy mountain in case some sort of catastrophic event happens—you know, like in case of a nuclear war or something—and all of a sudden all of the vegetation on the planet and everything gets wiped out and they have to rebuild the ecosystem from square one. And Oddvar, the guy who basically runs this shit on the day-to-day, is OBSESSED with me! I don't mean any disrespect when I say that—like, he's actually a really, really cool dude—but it's just like, aside from looking after the seeds and doing research and shit, Oddvar spends most of his time, like, being a *fan* of *me*. That's what he DOES. And I don't just mean that he knows all of my records by heart, or like, he has all the signed memorabilia or something like that. I mean, he DOES have all that shit, but it's deeper than that. He's a *scholar* of my life. He's like, a *student* of my world. He could almost write this book better than I could.

I remember when I met him, my reaction was just

like: WHAT? LOL. Like, it wasn't even like I was scared or something or like I was freaked out. I was just sort of like, taken aback, you know? I mean, the way he was talking to me about my life and like, all my shit, it was just like, there was almost this very *clinical* vibe he had. He wasn't shaking with excitement or like, trying to touch me or screaming his head off or anything. It was almost like, I mean, it was almost like actually seeing me in the flesh wasn't all that different from reading about me or watching videos or listening to the albums. He actually sort of talked to me like a person, which I totally wasn't expecting. I think because he was just so familiar with me and like, so deep in my world, actually meeting me wasn't that surprising for him.

The whole reason I even met him in the first place was that he won this contest on the radio station in Oslo where they were doing a trivia thing ahead of my concert there. He must've called into the contest from the seed vault on Spitsbergen, and he obviously knew more about me than anyone else, and so the prize for the contest was that the winner got to come backstage after the concert and hang out with me, and I don't know, I think there must have been some sort of charity component or something or else I probably wouldn't have agreed to it. But anyway, Oddvar came backstage, and like, we started talking, and I was sort of expecting it to be the normal kind of shit, you know—I mean, honestly, I was expecting a fourteen-year-old girl—but here comes this like, well-dressed, kinda intellectual-looking dude, who's like, thirty-six and doesn't look like a crazy person at all, and he was so *calm*, you know? He was so gracious and nice.

And like, I asked him a few questions, just trying to be nice, and he kinda blew me away with how much he knew. He started rattling off facts about my middle school, and like, all of the different producers I had worked with, and like, my vocal range, and then sort of the craziest thing about the encounter was that he just started asking *me* questions, but like, they weren't the kinds of questions that most fans would ask. It was more like—I mean, honestly, it felt like the whole point of meeting me for him was to fill in the gaps in his knowledge, you know? Like, he was almost treating me like I was research material, or like I was a very rare book about the Civil War or something and he was finally going to get the answers that he had been searching for after all these years of studying me. He didn't care about the *fact* of meeting me so much as he saw meeting me as the ultimate opportunity to answer the questions he couldn't answer without me. And, I mean, honestly, it was wild, because we were just supposed to hang for, like, half an hour or something—I think that's all that the radio station had promised him—but I ended up hanging out with him all night. He came out to dinner with us and like, we all had drinks together—he didn't really drink much, but we got him to take a shot or two—and after a few hours, like, *he* left early. *He* was the one who ended up saying to me: I have to be up early tomorrow for my boat ride back to Spitsbergen, but it has been a pleasure meeting you. And then he just disappeared. LOL. All he asked for was my email address, which I gave to him, of course, and he was like: Would it be all right if I contacted you in the future with questions about your work? And I was like: Yeah man, of course, this was dope. And that was it.

He emailed me the other day, actually. I guess he heard I had signed a deal to write this book, and he was like: Congratulations, my friend. I'm very much looking forward to reading the finished product.

I'd actually be really interested to hear what he has to say about it, you know, because in a way, like, this book is meant for *him*. I mean, I have no idea what I'm doing here. I just sit down every once in a while and try to knock out some pages that feel honest, you know, that express something truthful, but the best thing that could come of all this is that someone like Oddvar thinks it's dope.

One thing I was thinking about recently is like: This will be the first thing I've ever created that people can't play in the background, you know? If you're reading this book, *you're reading this book*. That's what you're doing. It's not like it's just gonna start playing over the sound system while you're in the frozen yogurt shop or like, waiting for the dentist or whatever. I mean, sure, yeah, someone could use the book in a way that it wasn't intended for—they could use it as a doorstop or like, kill a spider with it—but the only way you're really gonna *experience* the book is if you sit down with it and read it.

With music, it's like, sometimes that shit is just forced on you. Sometimes, you'll be in a restaurant, and you'll be eating with this girl, and they've got music playing in the background, but you haven't noticed it because the two of you are vibing, and, like, you're having this next-level conversation and you're feeling pretty good about where the night is headed, and then, all of a sudden, like, one of your songs comes on, and the whole restaurant turns around and looks at you. They've all known that you've been there the whole time. Like, obviously, they all tracked that you were there when you first walked in, but they've been cool about it up until now, because, you know, when you're in that kind of restaurant, the people eating there don't really freak out that easily over celebrities, or at least, like, they're rich enough or "in the scene" enough to know that that wouldn't really be a good look for them. But now your song is playing over the sound system, and *you're right there*, and so they can't hold it together anymore. Everyone feels like they just have a total pass to turn around in their chairs and stare at you like: What's he gonna do? What's gonna happen? And it's like: What are they expecting, you know? Do they think I'm gonna start singing along? Do they think I'm gonna get up on the table and do the dance routine from the video? But you know, that's music. That's what it's like to put sounds out into the world.

I don't want to get too dark or whatever, because I don't like to think about this kind of shit *at all,* but I remember this article came out a while ago where like, the CIA or the FBI or something—I forget exactly who it was, but it was one of those agencies—someone who used to work there leaked this list of all the songs they used to play to torture people. They'd like, blast these songs into the cells of people they were holding on an aircraft carrier or whatever in the middle of the ocean, and they'd just play the same song on full volume 24/7 for a month or a year, hoping that they'd break the guys down. And thank God none of my songs were on that list, but I knew a bunch of people's that were. My boy Scaggs, for instance, had a track on that list, and it really fucked him up for a while. Scaggs just like, couldn't even listen to that song anymore. He completely stopped playing it at his concerts—I think he even had his lawyer, like, try and sue whatever agency it was that was using it because he was so shaken up by the whole thing—and he even had to go into therapy for a while just to sort through how he was feeling about everything. And this is *Scaggs* we're talking about, you know? Like, this is a hard dude. This is a dude, who's like, been in the game since forever, and like, he's seen a BUNCH of shit. But the fact that his song was being used that way, it was just like: How could someone *do* that, you know? How could someone think that was possible?

But you learn after a while that you just can't control that shit. You can't control how your shit's gonna be used. You just leave your shit behind, and whatever people wanna do with it, that's their business. That's completely outside of your control.

At the place where I get my haircut, they just have the radio going all day, like full blast, and sometimes, I'll be sitting in the chair and like, two, three, four of my songs will come on over the course of my haircut, and Francisco, the guy who cuts my hair, will like, sing along to every one of them just like he sings along to all the *other* songs on the radio. He knows the words to EVERY song—like, every song on the top 40—and it's not even totally clear to me if he knows that those are MY songs he's singing, you know? I'm not even totally sure he knows that he's singing *at all*. For him, like, the music isn't even something he's *listening* to. It's more like *air*, you know? It's like air conditioner. It's the basic structure of his environment.

So you can't expect people to experience your music or like, think about your music the way you do, because people have all different kinds of reasons for listening, and at the end of the day, it's just a bunch of fucking sounds. No one can control that.

But it's a little harder and it hurts a little bit more when it's personal. Like, when it's about YOU and your life and your family and your friends and it's not about your songs, it's a little harder to sit back and deal with it when people say stuff or think stuff that you just KNOW isn't true, because then it's like: Well, I'm not leaving ME behind, you know? *That's* not part of the deal. You can do whatever you want with my songs, but you can't just do whatever you want with ME.

For example, nothing has brought more bullshit into my life than my relationship with Bob Winstock. Nothing. And I don't mean to say that my *actual* relationship with Bob has brought any bullshit into my life—if anything, he's brought me more clarity and perspective than, like, anyone else on the fucking planet—but the way people react to it and the way people deal with it is just like: What the fuck, guys? How can you possibly have an opinion about this?

I've seen what people say about him. I've read the articles. I know all the headlines: "Winstock Is a Bigot." "Winstock Is a Crazy Person." "Winstock Is a Dangerous Man." And every time I see that, it's just like: Do you people even know what you're *talking* about? I mean, I KNOW Bob. Bob and I have had *conversations*. LOTS of them. And he's honestly one of the warmest, kindest, most intelligent people I know.

Bob dropped backstage after my show a few years ago in Tampa, and he introduced himself, and he was like: Yo, I'm a fan. And I was like: Hey, man, I've heard a lot about you. And he was like: Forget it. Forget everything you've heard. Let me take you out for a meal and we can *actually* get to know each other.

And so he did. And we didn't go anywhere fancy or anything—we just went to like, a neighborhood joint, like Bob's favorite neighborhood spot where they serve Cuban food—and we were eating this next-level garlic chicken, and Bob looked me in the eyes and said: When was the last time somebody really TALKED to you? And there's just a way Bob looks at you, you know? Like, even more than what he's actually saying, just the way Bob looks at you is so . . . human. It's like Bob really sees you, creature to creature. And I just thought about the question he had asked me, and in my head I was just like: Never. I can't even remember.

And so we started talking about everything. Bob told me about his childhood—he had a really *rough* childhood—and I told him about growing up, you know, what it was like to be grinding since I was twelve, shooting up into the stratosphere and looking around and being like: Yo, is anyone up here with me? Am I all alone up here? And Bob just listened. I mean, it's not like he blew my mind or anything with what he was saying, but he just listened to me. He just made me feel heard. And at the end of it, when I was telling him about my music and the new direction I was trying to take it in, Bob was just like: Let me ask you something. And I was like: Yeah, man, anything. And he was like: What do you really want to be saying with your music? What do you actually want to be singing about? And I thought for a long time, and then I was just like: The world, man. Humanity. The whole crazy thing. And Bob looked at me for a second, and then he was like: So what's stopping you?

And I thought about it, and then I was just like: Nothing.

LOL.

Nothing.

After my song with Deez dropped, my whole shit basically changed. You know, I had gone from being a kid entertainer to being, like, an entertainer who happened to be fifteen. People were still adjusting themselves to it—it's not like there was this instant realignment in how people thought of me—but I could feel it in myself, you know, and that's what mattered. I was beginning to feel like an artist—like, a full-on artist—not just this kid who showed up for interviews and video shoots, but a full-blown artist with something to say.

And, meanwhile, my dad was feeling, like, obviously really shitty about the whole thing. I mean, first of all, I had just done this shit without even telling him, you know, like, he didn't even know the song existed, and now all his careful plans for how he was going to roll out the next phase of my image were just totally shot. He just thought

I was making, like, the biggest mistake of my career—he was so locked into the idea that he had it all figured out—and so he was convinced that this new sound was gonna be the worst possible thing that could happen to us. And then it only got worse when he realized that people were loving it.

At first people were sort of going like: Oh my god, I can't believe this is happening, oh my god, this is so crazy, and it was unclear if they were like, making fun of it or if they really dug it, but Deez and I kind of knew that whatever they were feeling, it was good. Even if they didn't know it yet, they were slowly adjusting themselves to the new reality we had set up for them. And eventually, like, in a matter of weeks, it was clear just from the way people were talking about it that like, they actually thought the song was dope and they actually understood that I was becoming a different artist from the one they thought they already knew, and once that happened, my dad was like *done*, you know? He was really embarrassed and bitter.

The way I saw it, I was *saving* him a lot of embarrassment, because if we had actually gone through with his plans—like, if we had actually released the album he wanted to release—it would have come out, and people would've thought it was lame or just, you know, kind of unremarkable, and then that would be that. We wouldn't be *done*, necessarily, but like, we definitely wouldn't be in a good position to capitalize on all the good vibes we had from the first album. But I think in his mind, like, he would've rather failed and still be the driving force behind the thing than succeeded and not have a say. It was just so clear from the way he reacted to everything that what ultimately mattered to him was control. And I kept telling him, like: This is dope, Dad! This song is blowing up. We're killing it. But he was just like: There is no WE. You've decided that I'm not part of the team anymore. And that was really fucking hurtful, to be honest.

I mean, you gotta remember, like, I was *fifteen*, you know? My dad was acting like we were *equals*, and it's like, yeah, okay, I mean, we had a professional relationship, but also, like: I was a *teenager*. That's the age when *everyone* hurts their parents. That's the age when *everyone* does kind of fucked-up, inconsiderate shit. But because of the position I was in, and because of the relationship we had, my fucked-up inconsiderate decisions had real effects on my dad's sense of self-worth, and that was honestly more than I was equipped to deal with at that point.

I mean, this is all shit I understand *now*, like, this is all shit I can talk about with a clear head *now*, but at the time, I was just really shitty about it, and I handled things maybe in a way that didn't help the situation. My dad was really shitty too, no doubt about it, but like, I said some really hurtful, like, really inconsiderate shit, and so I'm not saying for a second that the whole fallout was his fault. It was a two-way street, one hundred percent.

The worst it got was when I went over to my parents' house for dinner a few weeks after the song dropped, and it all kind of came to a head.

At that point, I was living on my own. My house was still in my parents' name, because like, no one will rent a house to a fifteen-year-old, but I had my own place a few minutes from theirs that was totally mine to do what I wanted with, and so for all intents and purposes, I was independent. But we still had a tradition where every Sunday night, I'd go over to their place for dinner and we'd all like, be a family together. We wouldn't have a chef or anything, and my mom would just cook, and we'd help her, and we'd like, bake some cookies and just try to be normal, do normal shit.

And so a few Sundays after the song came out, I went over to their place for dinner, and I was in the middle of helping my mom make a chicken potpie when my dad came down the stairs and was just like: Here you go.

And I looked at his hands, and he was holding this piece of paper, and at the top of it, it said "Separation Agreement." And I looked at it, and I was like: What the fuck, Dad? What is this? And he was like: You don't trust my judgment, you don't communicate with me, we can't work together anymore. And I was like: Why are you being like this? And he was like: I thought we were doing this thing together. I thought we were a team. And I was like: You're my dad! You're my manager! And he was like: If you're gonna treat me like I don't have anything to contribute, you might as well get a different manager. And I was like: Dad . . . And he was like: And maybe get a different dad while you're at it.

And that was like, I mean, you can imagine what hearing something like *that* felt like. My mom stopped chopping carrots, and she just looked at him, and she was like: Richard! My dad's name is Richard. And he knew he had crossed a line—like, he knew he had really gone overboard—but he already went there, you know? He wasn't gonna back down now. And so he just dug in his heels and doubled down, and he was like: My son wouldn't do this to me.

And I was just so hurt, you know? Like, I was just so upset about the whole thing, because I was just feeling like: What the fuck? Like, I thought this was what he wanted, you know? I thought this was what we both wanted for each other—to be killing it for as long as we could—and so I just went the fuck off on him. I just told him everything I was thinking. I just railed into him for being so pathetic and for living vicariously through me and for being so out of touch and for being so petty and for resenting his own son for his success and for being such a narcissist and for being such a shitty dad and for only ever really caring about me because he knew I had something that he needed and then hating me for exactly the same reason. And he was so pissed off that he just, like, didn't even say anything. He just calmly, like, swallowed something in his throat, and then he walked out the door and drove calmly away from the house. And I was so upset that I did the same thing. My mom was there with all the potpie shit all over her hands, like, crying and shit, and I just, without even saying anything to her, walked out the door and called up Trick Hatz to see if he wanted to get blazed. And when I got to Trick's house, he rolled us this like, perfect joint. Trick knows how to roll joints that are just like—they look like they come out of a machine, you know? They look like he went to school for it. And so I just sat back on Trick's patio chair and stared off into the mountains and got high.

• • •

And it was actually around that time that Bob came into my life.

Looking back on it now, the timing was sort of perfect—out goes one father figure, in comes another—but at the time, it didn't really occur to me. My dad and I had our falling-out, and a month or two later, Bob and I had that first conversation at the Cuban place, and pretty soon after that, he sent me some of his books to read, and I just started to get in DEEP, you know? I just went ALL IN.

About a week or so after we saw each other that first time, the books just showed up at my place in this plain brown box with a little note from Bob on the top that said: "Here's to many more beautiful conversations." And there were so many of them in the box that I didn't know where to start, so I just grabbed one at random and started reading. And that's pretty much what I was doing the whole time I was touring with the second album. It was almost like, I mean, I don't know, it was almost like I kind of stopped wanting to do anything else in between shows—I didn't really want to go out with Deez and the crew after a gig, and like, I didn't really want to play video games at the hotel anymore, and I didn't even want to watch shows or anything on my computer. I'd just order in some room service and find a nice chair and bury my head in one book or another. And slowly, gradually, I could feel my whole world changing.

I think a lot of it was like, I didn't really get much of a chance to *go to school*, you know? Like, yeah, legally I was required to have tutors go on tour with me, but those people are as much teachers as, like, the doctor who gave me my weed prescription in L.A. back in the day is a doctor. It's like: I'm sure he went to *medical school,* but at the end of the day, I don't think I'd want him *operating* on me.

So it was only really when I encountered Bob that I started to enter into anything like the *intellectual world.* I mean, I wasn't gonna get to go to *college.* That wasn't in the cards for me. But with Bob, like, I felt like I had someone who not only thought I was smart or who wanted to talk to me about real shit, but like, who sort of took it upon himself to create a program of study for me—a course of learning.

And so that's why when people jump to conclusions about Bob and what he stands for, it just makes me want to scream, because, like, how can you look at this man and look at his work and not see the total beauty of it? How can you just focus on one thing without even READING the book that contains it? How can you read some fucking ARTICLE and make up your mind about a complex human thinker?

I think hands down, the thing that Bob said that people just can't get behind is this comment he made about gay people. For most people, like, that's where it begins and ends with Bob. And I mean, here's what I know: Bob is not a bigot. I know in the core of my being that Bob loves and accepts all people. I don't necessarily agree with everything he says—like, I'm not some fucking *hype man* for Bob Winstock—but the dude is *not* some fucking hateful person who judges anybody for who they love or what they do with their lives. And it's really sad for me to see people take him out of context, because like, with the internet and everything, people just jump to conclusions when they've heard one little sound bite, and then it's like, they think they can condemn a person's entire life, their entire worldview, just from this one little thing. Like, they think that just because all these uber-right-wing, uber-intense dudes think of Bob as like, their *intellectual guide* or whatever, that must mean that Bob's ONE of them. And it's like: People have been interpreting philosophers and thinkers and doing whatever the fuck they want with them *forever*. This is nothing new. You can't just nail Bob down to the worst things that people do with his work and then go: Boom! Gotcha!

But okay, since we're here and since we're talking about Bob, like, let's get into it. Let's see how bad this thing really is.

To the best of my understanding, Bob's position on gay people is this: They're not natural. Everybody says it's natural to be gay, and Bob is like: No. They are a product of the modern world. They could only exist in a perverted society. Gay people are a response to a world that's out of whack.

I mean, is Bob saying we should *kill* all the gay people? No. And *I* definitely don't think that. I love gay people. I love all kinds of people. I mean, what people do in the privacy of their own homes, like, what people do with their own lives—why should that affect me? It's everyone's responsibility to figure their own shit out for themselves, and like, make their own way through the world, and what the fuck do I care who fucks who or how they do it?

But people are so hungry to like . . . throw each other into the fire, you know, so when they heard that Bob said that—which is like, crammed into chapter fifty-six of like, a *five-hundred-page book* he wrote SIXTEEN YEARS ago, but whatever, I mean, I guess he published it, so it's all fair game—but when that shit surfaced, all of a sudden people are asking me in interviews, like: Do YOU think gay people are not natural? Have YOU spoken to Bob about this?

And I'm like: That's not what Bob and I talk about! LOL. Look at all the OTHER shit Bob said. Look at all the actually amazing, like actually mind-blowing shit that he's written about, and actually READ his books, and then talk to me. I mean, seriously, it's like, if people actually *read* Bob, they'd have a lot more interesting shit to be angry about. I mean, Bob's said some shit that pokes at the very structure of our REALITY. But, meanwhile, they want me to focus on the gay shit? They want me to focus on THAT? They want me to spend my time on THAT just because that's what THEY'RE concerned about?

And again, it's like, this is something I really firmly believe: I think one of the things that normal people just absolutely can't understand about someone like me is that I just don't have the same framework for the world that they do. Even *intellectuals* or whatever, like, even really smart people, I mean, they may be *people of the world,* you know, but they're still essentially tied down to certain traditions—like, they're all still speaking from a certain POSITION in society—and so there's a real limit to how much they can understand. But for me, it's like, I have fans all over the world, you know—I exist for EVERYONE—and so I can't just be so quick to speak from a certain perspective. I go to places I've never even heard of, and they're using me to sell baby shampoo.

They're playing my songs at protests. They're dressing up as me for Halloween and putting ornaments of my face on the Christmas tree.

There are certain countries in the world—countries where like, I have *millions* of fans—where it's just straight up *illegal* to be gay. It's just like, not allowed. And like, what? I'm gonna say that that entire country is wrong? I'm gonna be vibing with all these people from that country at a concert one night and like, chilling with their president the next morning, and then back in the U.S., back on home soil, I'm gonna be like: Yo, that government is fucked up and those people need to get their shit together. Who the fuck am I? How can I possibly judge people like that? When we're all in the room together, I'm ONE OF THEM, you know? I'm a part of that society.

I play in places where they just chop off women's heads with swords. Seriously! That's what happens! I play in places where you can't use Google or whatever. And like, yeah, that sounds crazy to me, but like, what? I'm gonna be so arrogant that I'm gonna come out and be like: I'm taking a stand. This shit is wrong.

What the fuck? Who AM I?

I remember I was gonna play this concert in Tel Aviv, you know, in Israel, and like, all these activist groups were passing around this petition like: Yo, you can't play there, yo, you gotta show your support for the Palestinians by not playing a concert there. And I was just like: Do you people even understand how this WORKS?

When you ask me to do that shit, like, what you're asking me to do is to basically nail myself down to a certain number of principles that *you've* decided RIGHT

NOW, in the context of YOUR WORLD, are the most important principles that a person can have. And I get it. Like, I get that for most people, their context is really important. They've gotta use that shit to guide their decisions. But for me, like, and I'm not trying to sound self-important or something, but for me, I'm just operating on a different plane. I'm flying here and there and there and there, and I'm living for tomorrow. I'm trying to see the whole picture. That's honestly the biggest thing I'm working on all the time, like: How can I expand my perspective? How can I see MORE?

And so that's why it upsets me so much when people gang up on Bob because of this thing he said or that thing he said, because the idea that Bob has hatred for a certain type of people is just so fucking offensive. If Bob is saying something about gay people, he's not trying to put them down or to talk shit about them—he's just saying what he thinks. He's talking about what he's observed, the conclusions he's come to, and just because he's not saying the generally ACCEPTED thing where YOU come from doesn't make him some kind of monster or some kind of super-villain. Maybe you just need to step out of your frame of reference, take off the specific glasses that you've been wearing, and try to hear where he's coming from. Maybe then you'll understand him.

I just wish people would greet things with curiosity and openness instead of always with judgment, you know? Because it would be dope if people would admit sometimes that they don't know anything about anything. It feels so fucking amazing to admit that you're a total fucking idiot, because, like, we can't even understand what's going on in our *own hearts*, you know? We can't even understand how our *own minds* work. And now you've got something to say about *global politics*? Now you've got something to say about *the structure of the universe*? Sit down, bro. No one's asking you.

That was always the main problem with my dad, you know? He just couldn't admit the limits of his own understanding. Having even a little bit of success at all was the worst thing that could've ever happened to him, because, like, he didn't have it in him to be flexible. He didn't have it in him to assess the new situation and change. And that's what's required if you want to stay in the game. That's what you've gotta do if you wanna stick around. I mean, sure, yeah, it's great to have a plan, and like, it's great to think things through really far before you get going, but once you're out in the world, like, once the train is moving, it's just not *yours* anymore, you know? You can write an amazing TV show, and like, you can have all these plans for the whole series, but if everyone's like: Oh my god, we love this character, oh my god, we're gonna make all these memes about him, and you were planning on killing him off at the end of season one, that's just not an *option* anymore. You're not *allowed* to kill him. And you've gotta get to a place in your mind where, like, that's *dope*, you know what I'm saying? You've gotta fully embrace the influence and be happy about it and realize that your life doesn't just belong to you anymore: You're collaborating on it with the world.

But for some people, that kind of attitude just isn't possible, and I think, unfortunately, my dad was one of those people.

. . .

After that blowup at my parents' house, I didn't talk to him for a while. I would go and visit my mom, but whenever I'd show up over there, my dad would be gone, like, nowhere to be found, and I'd ask my mom, like: Yo, what's up? Where is he? And she'd just be like: He needs some time. He's in a very rough place right now.

We were both still really mad at each other. My mom was trying to repair things between us—like, she kept trying to get us in the same room or like, organize a family meeting or whatever—but I was really busy, and my dad was really mad, and so we would always find excuses to avoid each other.

My mom started this email thread with the three of us called "Family," and she sent us this long email being like: Guys, come on, you're father and son, you love each other, you built this beautiful thing together: Why can't you just make up? But whenever my dad would write on the thread, it was really short and kind of rude. He'd say he was interested in us all getting together, and he'd propose a time that worked for him, and then I'd be like: Sorry, I gotta do an interview at that time. Can we do this day instead? And then he just wouldn't respond.

And I had a new manager at that point. She's still my manager today: Shari. Part of me thought that it was just gonna be a temporary thing until my dad and I were ready to heal the wound, but this other part of me kind of knew that it was for good. At that point, like, my shit was blowing up even bigger than it did with the first album. I started steadily releasing all the tracks I had been recording with Trick and Deez and Bunny, and people were getting really excited about them, and I started to realize that, like, I pretty much already had the second album and now all that was left to do was put it all together and release it.

Deez had sort of become the main producer, and basically every day I was going over to his place and laying down new tracks and tweaking old ones and just working out the sound, you know, refining the thing. The album didn't have a concept, but it definitely had a sound, and it was a little more edgy than the first one. I mean, I don't think it was like, HARD or something—like, it wasn't some Scaggs shit—but I was definitely being honest about what my life was like, and like, the sound of the music reflected that. The album my dad and I did together had this very bright, like, very enthusiastic sound, and this new sound was more like, *swagger*, you know? That's the best way I can describe it.

So I was in the middle of finishing that up and doing press and playing the new songs at radio stations and going on late-night shows, and I didn't really realize that my mom and my dad were drifting apart too. I could kind of feel it whenever I'd go hang out with my mom. When my dad would come up, my mom would always sort of make this face like she was trying to smile and come off as though this was just a hard thing we were going through as a family and of course it would pass, but I guess what was really going on was like, our fight had sort of unleashed a lot of the worst parts of my father that had been put to bed by all of our success, and now *that guy* was coming back—that guy that my mom could never really stand—and unless he was going to do something about it, the strain was gonna be too much to take.

And then one day I went over to my parents' place, and my mom and I were like, sitting in the backyard by the pool having some barbeque that this Polynesian chef had prepared for us, and I just flat-out asked her, like: What's the deal? How come Dad is never here when I come to visit? And she just looked at me with these sad eyes, and she started crying.

And when she told me they were done, I felt this wave of relief pass over me. At the time, my attitude was like: Fuck this guy, you know? He's being a whiny little bitch and he's acting like a total fucking loser, and my mom doesn't need that shit right now. My mom is such a loving, caring, amazing person, and she doesn't need all this negativity weighing her down. And so I was glad that she was gonna get a chance to see what it was like without him.

But this is my dad we're talking about, you know? He wasn't gonna go quietly.

He was like, intent to have some success outside of me, and so he took all the money that was his share of our whole thing together—which, like, you gotta remember, was a couple million bucks at that point—and he started developing other acts. He was just basically going around the country, like, going to college vocal programs, watching singing competitions on TV and all of that shit, and just finding people, flying them out to L.A. and like, basically training them to be pop stars, making these little bets on them and hoping they would pay off. He was essentially, I mean, he was essentially trying to find another me, but like, one that he could control. And I would hear about what he was doing because, you know, at that point, the tabloids had obviously picked up on my parents' divorce, and my dad had become this kind of joke. Like, all these memes were being made about him like, making fun of his desperate quest to prove that he could do something without me, and like, every bet he made just lost. Every person he tried to groom into his perfect little Frankenstein performer just never panned out.

And then finally, like, a year or so after I released the second album—which fucking killed by the way—in the middle of probably the greatest time in my career so far up to that point, I read online that my dad had just gone totally bankrupt—he lost his entire share of our fortune. And at that point like, obviously, MY fortune had increased tenfold, but my dad had totally drained his piece of the original pie. And what I read online was that he was actually looking for work again—like, he was actually going around to radio stations and trying to be a sound engineer again—but nobody was hiring him because they had changed a lot of the equipment and it didn't work the same way anymore. Plus, like, everyone sort of knew who he was, and they didn't want to be associated with that kind of embarrassment.

And so I just thought, like: Okay. I've gotta reach out to him. Like, I've gotta look out for my dad. I'm not gonna let him STARVE over some beef between us about some songs I made with fucking Deez Soundzz. And so I called his cell phone—he hadn't changed his number—and he picked up, and I was like: Hey, Dad, what's up? Where are you now? And he was like: Hey, kiddo, I'm in New Mexico. And I was like: Oh, cool. What are you doing there? And he was like: I don't know. I don't know. And I was like: Okay, well, why don't you come back to L.A.? Let me put you up for a bit? And he was like: Yeah. Okay. I'd like that. And I was like: Dope. Perfect. I'm buying you a plane ticket right now. And he was like: Okay. I love you, kiddo. And I was like: Great, yeah, I love you too. And he was like: How's your mother doing? Is she okay? And I was like: Yeah, yeah, she's doing great. And he was like: Is she seeing anybody? Is she dating? And I was like, in my head, like: Shit, okay, I guess I have to tell him. And he was like: *Hmm?* How's she doing? And I was like: Yeah, Dad, she's, um . . . She's actually getting married again. And he was like: What? What are you talking about? And I was like: Yeah, she's getting married. It's not public yet, but it's happening. And he was like: Whoa. Shit. Who's she marrying? And I was like: Let's talk about it when you get here. I'm psyched to see you. And he was like: Come on, man, who? And I was just like: Fuck, man, I really don't wanna get into this right now. And he was just like: WHO? Who? And I was just like: Bob. Bob Winstock. She's marrying Bob Winstock. And then he hung up the phone.

LOL.

Believe me, I was just as shocked as anybody when it first started happening. When I introduced the two of them, I wasn't thinking about that *at all*. I didn't even consider it a possibility. I was just like: Here's two people who are super-important in my life—why don't they meet and become friends? And even though we were all vibing at that first dinner we had together, I had no idea that like, *that* was gonna happen.

I mean, I love it. I think they're absolutely great together. It's like I said, you know, Bob has this way of just listening to you—he's super grounded and human—and I think my mom really needed someone like that. Especially after all the shit with my dad, she just needed someone who was confident and self-assured and had his own thing going on, and more than anything, you know, I think she needed someone who would actually be *available* to her, you know? Someone who had the space to look at her and be with her and be like: What's going on with YOU? What's happening inside of YOUR head? So I'm not surprised that they got along so well. My mom and I are very similar, ultimately—I think we respond to the same kinds of things in people.

Not to mention, like, it's super-hard for someone like my mom to date, because everyone's a total freak about who her son is. I mean, yeah, it's hard for me to really meet people and have an honest conversation with them, but like, it's also really hard for my mom—maybe even harder—because all these people sort of glob onto her when they find out who she is, and they don't even want to talk to her about HER, you know? They just want to talk to her about this person she's connected to. It's like they think she's an *extension* of me—like she's my regional office. And at least when they're doing that shit to me, I'm still the focus of their attention.

So, a little while after that first dinner together, I started to hear from Bob or my mom that they were having lunch together, and then I'd hear they were going out to coffee, and then I'd hear they were having dinner just the two of them or like, going on a hike up in the Santa Monica Mountains, and eventually I was just like: Guys, what's going on here? I sort of confronted them about it when we were all hanging out together at my place. And they both sort of smiled, like, a little embarrassed, and they were both sort of looking at each other like: What do we say? And I was just like: Whoa, really? And they both just sort of looked at me, like: Is that okay? And I was just like: Of course! Wow. Amazing.

And it was actually super-cute, you know? I mean, my mom was just so happy—like, I'd honestly never seen her so in love the whole time she was with my dad—and Bob was just like a little boy. Here was this incredibly intelligent dude, this guy who's sort of my guru, and I just got to see him, like, smiling and blushing like a little kid with a crush. And they were clearly so relieved to tell me, you know, because I think they were worried about how I might react. I think they were worried it might make me uncomfortable, or like, I might want them to stop. But, of course, I was all for it. I mean, I was worried about what would happen if they broke up or ended up hurting each other, but it was pretty clear after a while that they were both in it for the long haul and that they weren't taking any of it lightly. You know, my mom had been divorced from my dad for almost a year now, and Bob had been married a few years back, and so this wasn't their first rodeo. They both knew how to navigate the waters.

And it's crazy, because like, at the same time Bob and

my mom were starting to get serious, I was going through my own sort of whirlwind relationship stuff with Mandy.

She had decided at that point that she probably wasn't a lesbian, and so we got back together, and it was good for a while—like, it was really, really good—but then we just started having major problems—like, deep, unfixable problems—and there was a lot of love there, but it started to become clear to both of us that like, something just wasn't right.

The first sort of crack started to show when Mandy showed me this new track from her upcoming album—this was *Heartache/Heartbreak*—and she asked me to be on it. I don't know if I'm supposed to talk about this, but the track was "North Star"—you know, the one she ended up doing with Brett Andrews—and Mandy came to me with it, and she was like: Hey, my people think it would be a good idea for us to collaborate on something together, you know, like, a love song that we could perform together at awards shows and all that shit. And I wasn't opposed to the idea necessarily, but I listened to the song, and I was just like: Whoa. LOL. This might be the worst song I've ever heard. I think I even said that to her. Halfway through the demo, I just started laughing and I was like: Turn it off, turn it off, and she was really hurt by that.

I mean, I don't think I was being *that* much of a dick—it's not like *she* wrote the song. It was probably one of those Australian dudes. I forget which one. I think it was like, Bogz or Da-LITER or someone like that, you know, one of those "New Aussie" people—but Mandy felt like it was a personal attack on her because she really liked it and she thought I was judging her for her taste, which like, I totally wasn't. I just thought the song was bullshit.

I mean, I don't mean to talk shit about Mandy at all, because like, I have a ton of love for her and I always will, but I just think at that time she had a sort of limited conception of what was possible as an artist. We both sort of came up as these "kid" musicians, you know, these "kid artists," and our sounds really weren't that different at the beginning, but my way out of that, like, my way of emerging from that was to do all that shit I was doing with Deez and Trick and Z—you know, like, the sort of more progressive, edgier, crazier stuff—and for Mandy that just wasn't really an option, you know, because like, how was she even gonna *hang out* with those people in the first place? It was one thing for those guys to be smoking weed and chilling in the studio with a fifteen-year-old BOY, you know, or like, drinking champagne and having all these girls in the jacuzzi with a fifteen-year-old BOY, but like, you can't do that shit with a GIRL because then you might actually go to JAIL. Like, a fifteen-year-old girl at your house party is just a liability for everybody. And so that kind of meant that Mandy was mostly still hanging out with her Kidz Spot crew, and the same team that was managing her through her first album was managing her through her second album, and so the sound just kind of stayed the same and so did the image. You know, like, every scene in her music videos would still just be her SMILING every time she looked at the camera, and like, dancing on the beach and singing with this fake backup band that she didn't even play with, and the whole thing just felt like an advertisement for an amusement park or something, you know? Like, that was the vibe she was on. It was like: It'll be fun for the whole family! And when I'd bring Mandy around to Deez's house or Trick's house, it's not like those guys were *mean* to her or anything—I mean, they actually really loved Mandy, and they all thought she was next-level talented—but the vibe would definitely change. All of a sudden, it was like I wasn't their younger brother who they were taking to the strip club for the first time or like, convincing some older girl to hook up with. All of a sudden, it was like: Whoa. There are two CHILDREN at our party. And that was really tough for Mandy to deal with.

It was especially shitty because her image and her sound and everything were all about *innocence*, you know—like, it was all so *wholesome* and *good* and *clean*— but the obvious next step for her, like, the obvious next phase of her career was for her to become "sexy" in one way or another. Like, everybody was pretending for the moment that she didn't have boobs and they didn't want to fuck her, but like, the SECOND she turned eighteen, like, the *literal moment* when the clock struck midnight, everybody was expecting her to drop some video where she was in a bra and panties and like, she was all lubed up with grease in a mechanic shop, humping a wrench and singing about some guy "fixing her up like a carbu- retor." But Mandy couldn't do that shit yet because it basi- cally would've been child porn, you know? Her team kept trying to come up with all this shit for her to do— like, they were trying to come up with stuff that was like, still hot and catchy and could still get people dancing but that wasn't too overtly sexual—but the result, to me, just

FAMOUS PEOPLE •

51

felt like lies. It just felt really dry and empty and manu-factured. And I mean, it *worked*—like, the fans still loved it, and they still played it on the radio, and Mandy still had a sold-out tour with *L.A. Baby* and *Heartache/ Heartbreak*—but I just kind of couldn't stand the music she was making. Honestly, I got the sense that neither could she. I mean, that was always the sad part to me: She has this next-level voice—like, honestly, Mandy has one of the best singing voices I've ever heard. It's like, actu-ally, technically perfect. And it's not just like she's natu-rally talented or something. I mean, she IS naturally talented, that's not even a question, but like, the thing about Mandy that I don't think a lot of people realize is that she's this incredibly skilled *musician*. You can give her a piece of sheet music, like, literally anything, and she can sight-read it for you first try. It doesn't matter if it's new shit or old shit or if it's even in her key. She can do it—but it just seemed at the time like she didn't really know WHY she was singing, you know? It seemed like she didn't really have a REASON. The dedication was all there, the work ethic was all there, but she didn't have any DIRECTION. She was like one of those kids who's crushing it in high school and getting straight As and playing the violin and like, joining all the clubs, and running track, and then like, if you ask them *why* any of this shit is important to them, they just look at you like: What the fuck are you *talking* about? And so whenever I'd be like: What kind of ARTIST do you want to be? What do you want to be singing about? she would always just get really pissed off and defensive.

Plus, like, on top of it all—and Mandy probably doesn't want me saying this, but like, whatever, I'll edit it out if she really asks me to—I think a big part of the reason we started to see that our thing wasn't going to work was that Mandy just couldn't stand Bob. I mean, they got along fine at first, you know, because Mandy's a really sweet person and she's not gonna be mean to anybody unless she decides that she doesn't like them, but Bob's kind of this no-bullshit guy—like, he just says what he thinks one hundred percent of the time—and so being around him, like, he demands everyone's full participation in every conversation, and I think Mandy just found it exhausting after a while.

I remember Mandy crying after this double date we had with Bob and my mom where she was like: He makes me feel so STUPID. And I just started laughing, and I was like: Bob makes EVERYONE feel stupid. Isn't it amazing? And Mandy was like: No! It makes me feel awful! And then she started telling me about how she was losing fans because of the shit Bob had said about gay people, and how she really didn't think it was a good idea that I was so closely associated with him, and I was just like: Shit. I'm gonna have to make a decision here. Like, I'm gonna have to choose between Mandy and Bob. And that honestly wasn't that difficult for me. Mandy's my girl for life, no question about it, but it was just so clear at that point that we were heading down different paths, and Bob was like, I mean, at that point, Bob was already my family.

Yo, but I'm realizing, it's pretty crazy that I've been writing this thing for as long as I have and I haven't even said anything about my security team!

I just thought about them, because, like, during all the shit with Mandy, I remember we would be fighting all the time in front of these dudes, and at a certain point, I remember looking at Patrick—that's one of my guys—after we dropped Mandy off at her house one night, and Patrick was just like: *Bro* . . . And the two of us just immediately started laughing like crazy. He almost knew before I did that things were going sour, you know, because he just spends his whole day, like, watching me, observing what's going on, so he's got a pretty clear picture of what's happening in my head.

I know it's their job to like, stay in the background or whatever and sort of keep a low profile, so I won't say too much about them, but it just feels insane that I spend so much of my time with these guys and I'm writing this book and I haven't even told you *anything*. I'm sitting here on the jet right now, looking around and taking a break from writing for a minute, and I'm realizing like: I hang with these people probably more than any other people in the world—they're the only ones who ride with me everywhere when we travel, they're the only ones who sleep in the house—and in a way, like, these guys are my closest friends. I'm not ashamed at all to say that: My security team are some of the most important people in my life.

First of all, let me just say that I never would've imagined when I started all this—like, it never would've crossed my mind when I was making those recordings with my dad back in St. James—that when I "made it," that would mean I'd be spending the biggest chunk of my time with these enormous dudes who used to be Army

Rangers and professional wrestlers and mob enforcers and Secret Service members. LOL.

Not to say that these dudes are scary. I mean, if you fuck with them, one hundred percent they'll get in your face, but I honestly have some of the best, like, coolest, most professional and hilarious and amazing guys protecting me on the day-to-day. I'd probably just be straight up dead without them. Seriously. I would've just like, exited my car one day and been torn to shreds by a bunch of crazy ten-year-olds in Argentina. That's how bad it was getting.

I first realized I needed a security detail when this woman tried to kill me in Australia.

I was doing this thing at a radio station in Sydney, and this was right when the first album dropped, you know, so we were still sort of adjusting to the magnitude of the thing we had created, and so we pulled up to the radio station, and like, yeah we were expecting a crowd, but when we got there, it was a fucking *army*. It was just me at that point and my dad and my road manager, Bobby, and like, I guess the person that the radio station had sent with us to come pick us up at our hotel, and the second we opened the door to the SUV, the whole crowd just MOBBED it. It was like they were a pack of zombies and we were the only people left in the world with fresh blood. And this fucking girl, like, this absolutely insane woman, just out of nowhere, comes rushing up to me and starts kissing me on the mouth. Like, they weren't *sweet* kisses or anything like that—she wasn't being cute about it. They were really aggressive, like, really violent kisses, like she was trying to suck a demon out of me or something. And remember,

I'm *fourteen* at this point, so I've hardly even kissed anybody in my life. And now here was this like, to my knowledge, fully grown woman, just *aggressively* kissing me and biting my neck and shit, and she looked like a fucking vampire. Like, if you had told me she had been exposed to some crazy chemical in a lab and that she was a mutant now, I'd believe you. She did not look human.

And my dad and Bobby were trying to pull her off of me, you know, and we were all kind of freaking out, and she took out this nail file and started swinging it around at everybody. I'm not even sure it was a nail file. In my mind when I remember it, I always think it was a little scalpel or something, you know? Like, what scientists use to scoop up a bit of sample?

And, thankfully, the guy who was riding with us from the radio station just socked her in the face. LOL. Like, it was some Street Fighter shit. He just shot his arm out and then, boom, she was out. But that really shook us all up. It took me a long time before I was even comfortable playing in Australia again.

So that's when Curt and Patrick came on board. At the beginning there was this other guy Steve too, but I had to let him go. I can't talk about the reason I fired him because we both signed this nondisclosure thing, but whatever. Dude was a fuck-face. Let's just leave it at that.

Curt and Patrick and Mo, on the other hand, are the real fucking deal. Mo got hired after Steve was gone. It was only once those dudes came into my life that I realized what it did to me, you know, being an only child.

I remember at his job interview, Patrick was wearing

this pro-wrestling shirt, and, you know, I think he was expecting to show up and I was gonna be this like, "girly-boy pop star" or whatever. Not that there's anything wrong with that. If you're a girly-boy, be a girly-boy, that's cool. But I saw Patrick's shirt, and it had the Bones on it, and I was like: YOOOO, it's the Bones! And he was like: Whoa, bro, you watch *Thursday Night Mayhem*? And I was like: Of course! BONE CRUSHER! And he just, like, picked me up right there in the middle of the interview and did the move on me, and my parents were looking at us like: What. The. Fuck. But I said on the spot, like: This guy's on the team. I want this guy protecting me.

And more than a lot of people in my life, Patrick's just been there for me when shit was tough. I mean, Patrick's this enormous dude, and like, he used to crawl around in the desert in Afghanistan shooting Al Qaeda guys or whatever, but he's an amazing listener. He's actually just such a sweet guy. And he sacrifices so much to be with me. He's got a wife and a daughter, and they hang around every once in a while—Gloria's awesome, and Amelia is like, the cutest little baby I've ever seen—but for most of his life, Patrick's just hanging out with me, watching my back. He's there at every concert, standing by the base of the stage, scanning the whole place with his eyes, looking out for trouble. And when it counts, he's there. Not just with the protection, but like, with his friendship.

I mean, I told you about the scene at the airport when I found out my dad was dead. Curt and Patrick and Mo just rushed me the fuck out of there. I don't even know how they were able to do it so fast: They just got me right into the car, and we were on the road. They knew that like,

I wouldn't want any cameras seeing me crying, and so it was just like, their adrenaline kicked in, and they made sure that everything that needed to happen happened. I mean, I guess that's the benefit of hiring all these military guys and sports guys is that they know how to perform under pressure. They make the impossible possible.

And it was only once we got into the Escalade and like, got the windows up and got going on the freeway that I even allowed myself to feel anything about what had happened. I mean, I *never* cry, you know? Like, I probably hadn't cried in ten years. I didn't even cry when Mandy and I split up. But now it was just like a fucking river. It was like a pipe had burst. It was like an anime movie or something. Just WAAHHHHHH. Like, those big animated tears flying everywhere like a sprinkler.

And Patrick, just like, without even making a big deal out of it or something just like, reached over and put his hand on my shoulder. He didn't say anything or like, give me a talk or whatever. He just like, put his hand on my shoulder and held it there, kind of firm. And, I don't know, I guess I just really needed that warmth, you know? I just really needed that human connection. I just curled up into Patrick's chest and he held me and rocked me back and forth, and I just cried, like, ten years' worth of tears into his enormous body.

Can I tell you a secret?

Everyone's been waiting for my fourth album—like, there's been all this speculation about what it's gonna be and when it's gonna drop and everyone's wondering what I'm gonna do next—but here's the thing:

It's not an album.

LOL.

It's a video game.

Nobody knows it yet—I mean, except for the people who are working on it—but the idea came to me about a year ago when I was thinking about what to do after *Roses and Mud.*

Basically, I was sort of like: Where do I go from here, you know? How do I top this?

And I sort of realized that like, at least for the time being, there were no more sounds I could create that were gonna top what I had just done. In order to move forward, I was gonna need to do something else, expand my conception of what I can do, and so I started thinking, like: How do I capture this feeling for people? How do I capture what it's like to actually be there in the room at a moment of major creative inspiration?

And that turned into a larger question of like: How do I capture what it's like to be *me*, you know? How can I share my life with people in the fullest possible way so that they can understand where I'm coming from and figure out what I'm all about?

And then it was like a lightbulb just went off in my head. I mean, seriously, it was like a movie or something. It was just like: YES. And I started figuring out who I knew in the gaming world and how I could get them to work with me.

Let me just say right off the bat, like: I'm not some

total *n00b* to gaming. Like, video games have been a pretty central part of my life since—I mean definitely since I was a kid—but especially since I became famous. They've been really important, just in terms of my sanity.

At least once a week since we went on tour with the first album, I've been going online and putting on the headset and playing *Urban Warrior* or *Lonely Vortex* or something like that, and it's amazing, because like, here I am, and I'm talking to people from all over the world, and I'm playing with them, and nobody knows who I am. Like, it's actually, legitimately, the only time in my life when I get to interact with normal people in a way that doesn't feel, like, hypercharged and inauthentic. And sometimes, back in the day, I would even tell people who I was. Like, someone would say that my voice sounded really familiar, or like, they'd start talking shit about one of my songs, and if I liked the person, like, if we were having a good time and I thought they were a good player, I'd be like: Yeah, well, actually . . . But ninety-nine percent of the time they didn't believe me. The one time this guy *did* believe me, he ended up posting my gamer tag online, and eventually I had to change it because like, it turned the video game world right back into the real world. All of a sudden, I'd try to join a match, and the second people would see my gamer tag pop up, they'd freak out and ask me to say stuff and like, yell shit at me or put me on speakerphone with their friends or call me a faggot and tell me to kill myself, and it got so bad that like, eventually, I just muted my headphones and turned off my mic and I tried to play the matches without any sound. But that kind of ruined it for me, you know, because the thing I really liked about it was the social aspect—like, just being part of a team, being one of the crew. When people knew who I was, all of a sudden the matches would come to a standstill because everybody would just want to crowd around my character and like, touch me with their guns and shit and take screenshots with the in-game camera, and I'd be running around trying to actually complete the objectives, you know, and everybody else—like, it didn't matter if they were on my team or on the other team—would just be following me around trying to get close to me. And when I'd kill someone, they'd be like: AWESOME! I can't believe it! And it was like: No! This is a GAME! You know? You've gotta actually PLAY! But, that's how crazy the world is. LOL. All these gamer kids turned into, like, the *virtual paparazzi*. My publicist even told me that there were websites willing to pay people a couple thousand bucks for pictures of my CHARACTER in *Urban Warrior*. Like, not even pictures of ME: pictures of my AVATAR, a bunch of fucking pixels that looked *exactly the same* as everybody else's fucking pixels. And it's like, yeah, okay, I guess I could see how it would be interesting to people to see how I customized my character or like, see what skins I wore or what guns I used, but like, at the end of the day, it's not like my guy looked THAT different from anybody else's. There aren't THAT many options in *Urban Warrior*. But still, all these videos would be posted of me playing, and then all these gaming commentators would be like: Yo! He sucks at this game! And it was like: Nobody else was even PLAYING, you know? How could anyone possibly be able to tell whether I sucked or not based on these bullshit matches? I don't know. I mean, I think it's funny now, but it actually kind of felt like a betrayal when that guy posted my gamer tag. We had been playing together for a while and like, we actually really LIKED each other, you know? We weren't FRIENDS or anything, but we had been placed in a few matches together, and there's this option in *Urban Warrior* where you can put certain players into your "preferred" category, and so we both put each other in that category, and for like, a couple months, we were playing together a lot. And while we'd be waiting for the map to load, we'd, like, chat about other games we liked to play, or like, talk about our favorite maps, or our favorite weapons, or where we were from, and then it was like, the SECOND I told him who I was, like, the second I opened up to him, he just turned into a fucking alien. He was like: WHAT?? I could literally feel through my headset how I had stopped being a person to him. We had been talking for months—I mean, literally MONTHS—about all kinds of shit, and then it was just like, the *moment* he found out who I was, all of that dropped away, and he couldn't even find the words. He was just like: AHHHHGHEKGHAEHGAHG!

And at first, I really didn't wanna change my gamer tag after he posted it, because I liked the name a lot, and like, it had all my stats and all my weapons and upgrades and shit, and in *Urban Warrior,* you can't change your name without creating a whole new profile, so I was really hesitant to do that because like, it takes a lot of time to build up all your skills and attributes again, but after a while, it just became too depressing to keep joining these games where I ended up having to yell at people to leave me the fuck alone, and so I created a new profile and started from Level One. And I won't tell you what my new gamer tag is, but it's super-fucking-normal. LOL. When I'm on the headset now, I'll kind of mask my voice a little bit so that no one can recognize me. Not too intensely, but like, I'll sometimes put on a Southern accent or like, an English accent or something, and so people will either think I'm this other person entirely, or they'll just assume I'm some random kid fucking around.

It's also worth mentioning that, like, before I started playing video games—like, before I started joking around with people on the headset—I had no idea that I was funny. LOL. Or I mean, I could never TRUST that I was funny, because in the real world, like, when I'm hanging out with a normal person—someone who works at a radio station or like, someone who works in my manager's office—everything I say to them is just *hilarious*, you know? If they even SENSE that I'm trying to make a joke, they've gotta LOL, because in their head, like, all that's going on is: Oh my god I'm talking to him oh my god I'm talking to him. Actually, the way most normal people talk to me is a lot like the way I used to talk to black people when I first moved out to L.A. LOL. I was meeting some of the first black people I had ever met—because like, St. James isn't exactly known for its diversity—and every time I was talking to one of them, all that would be going through my mind is just: Oh my god, I'm talking to a black person, oh my god, I'm talking to a black person.

But on the headset, you know, in the game, I can actually make people laugh, and like, I can actually have a fun time with them and feel like they like me just based on what I'm *saying*, so that's really grounded me over the years.

But, anyway, my idea for the game was that it was gonna be the story of my life—you know, like, basically, it's a role-playing game, and you're me, but starting from childhood, you get to make all these different choices—and everybody who plays the game ends up having a totally different experience depending on what they do.

You all start in the same place—the game begins in St. James Hospital with me being born—and the idea is that, you know, pretty much from that point on, you have all of these different options, and you can just become a totally different person.

And there's an option where you never post that video—you know, the one of me singing the national anthem—and so you never become famous.

And there's a whole option where you end up going to college and getting a normal job, or like, dropping out of high school and running away from home.

And there's an option where, for the second album, you just record all the songs that my dad had written for me and you never do all that shit with Deez.

And there's an option where you never break up with Mandy, and the two of you end up getting married.

And then there's this option where like, you make ALL the same choices that I made and you get to do basically exactly what I've done and like, you see what it's like for yourself—you feel like the choices are YOUR choices and it's YOUR life—and so you come out of the game maybe feeling like you understand me a little bit better.

And, obviously, like, you can customize all your tats

and hairstyles and wardrobes and all that shit. You can even like, go to the gym and get super-ripped. LOL. I've actually been using the game engine to test out new looks on myself before I try them in real life.

And I think what's cool about it, or like, what I'm trying to say with it, you know, is that none of this was written in the stars. Nothing in life is laid out for us ahead of time. At every stage, you know, at any point in time, we can always shape our own destinies. We can always be whoever we want to be. And a lot of the time, like, whoever ends up being one particular kind of person is just as random as whoever ends up being another particular type of person. It's just as random that I ended up being me as it is that you ended up being you.

And so the game is sort of this massive project, you know, and I don't really think I realized when we started it how long it was gonna take.

I'm working on it with this couple, Roger and Ines, who are these totally dope video game designers in San Francisco who met in grad school and got married and formed a little company together, and they're not the biggest or like, the most experienced designers in the world, but when I went to meet with them, they were the ones who were most enthusiastic about the idea and who actually thought we could pull it off, so they're the ones I ended up working with. The first game that they made is this little indie thing where you're a caterpillar who turns into a butterfly and then you fly around the city giving good luck to people. And I played that one, and it was super cute and creative, and I was like: Awww. I love these guys!

Actually, it was kind of crazy how most of the video

game people treated me when I talked with them. In a way, it was nice to be reminded that there are people who just don't give a fuck about me or my world because they've got their own, like, fully cohesive world that doesn't have anything to do with me, but for the first time in as long as I can remember, I was being *rejected*, you know what I mean? I was meeting with all these video game people and telling them about my idea, and they were all just sort of looking at me like: Why would WE do this? What's in it for US? And they all just basically told me: This idea won't work and it's going to be way too expensive and it's going to take way too much of our time and nobody is gonna play it. And a few of them asked me if I would do music for THEIR games—you know, like, the games they were already developing—but I was just like: Nah, I don't think so.

So I finally ended up meeting with Roger and Ines, and you know, I mean, I love them—like, they're the best—but I do sometimes wonder if they're in over their heads. LOL.

The hardest part, you know, is just that there are infinite possibilities, and we all want the world to feel as open as possible, but the bigger the world gets, like, the more expensive the game becomes to make. And, like, we don't have any big backers or anything—I'm kind of just financing the thing myself—so that's actually why I've been touring so much this year. I've gotta build up the revenue so we can keep chipping away at it.

Roger and Ines gave me an initial estimate for what they thought it was gonna cost, but we've already blown WAY past that, and now it's like, every couple weeks, they're going: Hey, we think we need a little bit more money. Hey, we're gonna need to hire another programmer.

But, whatever. I guess that's just how this shit works.

Everyone thinks it's a bad idea.

LOL.

Obviously, I've been keeping it under wraps from the general public, and like, so far it doesn't seem like there's been any leaks—I had my lawyer draw up these massive NDAs for everybody involved—but literally everyone I've talked to about it—my mom, Deez, my manager, Bob—all think that the project is pretty much doomed and that I'm just gonna fall on my face big-time.

But, you know, something happens when a bunch of people you love tell you not to do something one time and then you do it anyway and it turns out to be genius: The *next* time they tell you not to do something, like, the next time they voice their concerns, you just sort of look at them like: *Wellllll* . . .

When it comes down to it, no one else can make your decisions for you. They can give you advice, they can tell you what shit looks like from where they're standing, but you're the only person who's standing in your skin, so you're the one who's gotta make the call. It might make some people laugh, and it might make some people upset, and it might even make some people feel like they know better than you, but if you don't start living your own life, who will?

After that phone call with my dad, I didn't hear from him for a while.

I think he took it really hard. I mean, I *know* he did, because he basically broke off contact entirely after that, and then we sort of entered into what I've started to think of as the "dark period" where basically, like, my dad just fully lost his mind.

Thinking about it now, all I can do is laugh, but at the time, it was obviously really scary, and the whole thing just happened so rapidly. It was just like, before what was happening with him was sad, you know, but now it seemed like there had actually been a *break with reality*, and that was really fucking terrifying, to be honest. I mean, the tricky thing, you know, the thing that made it especially hard, was that he wasn't even returning my calls, so I just had to watch this all unfold from afar, and at first, it was kind of scary and like, I was really worried about him, but after a while, it just started to become *annoying*, you know? No one really tells you that about dealing with someone who's losing their mind: It's actually super-fucking-annoying most of the time, and you sort of end up hating the person. And like, yeah, okay, a part of me could recognize that this guy who was doing and saying all this crazy shit wasn't really my dad and that like, there was actually some little demon who had hunkered down inside him and was speaking and acting through him, but the lines kind of blurred sometimes because a lot of the shit he was saying just sounded like the kind of hurtful, awful shit that my dad had *always* wanted to say but didn't feel like he could.

It's hard to talk about my dad, you know, because there's obviously a lot of anger on my part, and like, I still kind of hate the guy, but also, I feel a certain level of responsibility for what happened. At a certain point, I decided that like, I was just gonna cut him out entirely and let him rot away on his own, because, like, he kept harming my life and my mom's life in his craziness, and I was just sort of like: This isn't my problem to deal with anymore. I'm not gonna let him drag me and my mom and my life and my music down with him in this spiral, because we've got too many places to go, and like, yeah, I was an asshole, yeah, I could've handled things better, but I tried to make things right, and he didn't even give it a chance, so like, fuck that guy.

But now, I don't know. There's a part of me that feels like if I had done a bit more, or like, if I had tried a bit harder, I could've prevented what happened, or like, I could've maybe even brought him back into my life, you know, and just changed the story entirely. I guess that's the thing about life: We never really know what's gonna happen until it happens, and once it happens, it's too late to do anything about it.

The first I heard from my dad after he dropped off the face of the earth was when he started his blog. After I told him about my mom and Bob, he stopped responding to me and he changed his phone number, and he started this blog that he would post to every once in a while, which was like, I guess just his general thoughts about the world. Like, at first it was kind of weird because he was sort of doing like, general music and pop culture reviews and op-ed pieces. No one really knew why he was doing it, but he just sort of positioned himself as like, a "pop culture commentator," I guess because he was thinking like: Maybe someone will pay me for this? Maybe I can have a second career as someone who does this kind of thing? And I'm guessing like, he read some article about all these teenagers who were starting fashion blogs and music blogs and then getting hired by these big media conglomerates to be staff writers, and so he thought, like: People already kind of know who I am, I'm already kind of a public figure. Why don't I give this a whirl? But, you know, the writing just wasn't that good. I mean, first of all, he had already kind of blown his credibility, and like, no one was really interested in taking him seriously as a commentator, and second of all, like, the writing itself was just *bad*. Like, you could never really figure out what his opinion was, and it was always just sort of like—I mean, in retrospect, it was the beginning of him losing his mind—but the writing was always a little disjointed and like, bad in that way that only crazy people's writing can be bad. There was this one article about *Heartache/Heartbreak* where he was just like, comparing Mandy to an *alligator* the whole time, and it was like: What the fuck are you *talking* about, you know? It was really weird.

So he was doing that for a while, and I was still trying to get in touch with him, but he wasn't responding to anything, and like, meanwhile, you know, I was helping my mom prepare for her wedding with Bob, which was going to be this very small, very beautiful thing in Buenos Aires, where, like, we had rented this whole little villa, and I was also touring and laying down some new tracks with Skelet0r, and so I just wasn't ultimately paying that much attention to what was going on with my dad.

And then he got the Web series, and that sort of changed the mood of the whole thing.

I mean, I'm sure a lot of you have seen it—I don't need to go into detail about the whole thing—but, it was just sort of fucked up, because like, Content Bucket *had* to have known that he wasn't doing well—like, they had to have met him and seen the state he was in and understood that he was a deeply unhealthy person—but they just didn't give a fuck. They just, like, wanted to cash in on whatever little viral thing those videos were gonna be, and so they basically gave him free rein to say whatever the fuck he wanted about me, and whatever the fuck he wanted about my mom and Bob and the world and then, you know, they'd put in all these ironic edits and like, do all this fucked-up, goofy shit around these videos of him, like, clearly losing his mind. And, you know, if you listen to those rants, they just make no fucking sense at all. At first, like, I thought my dad was in on the joke or something—like, I thought it was maybe this weird, ultimately unsuccessful attempt at some kind of "alt-humor" or whatever—but it was so clear after the first two or three videos that my dad was totally fucking serious and that the people at Content Bucket were just laughing their asses off in the editing room.

And then the stupidest fucking part, you know, the part that really pissed me off about the whole thing, was that the news would still report on these videos as if they were *actual* allegations that I needed to respond to, you know? Like, I'd get asked in interviews about this crazy conspiracy theory or that crazy conspiracy theory, and I'd just be like: Are you guys fucking serious? You're gonna ask me to respond to *this*?

And I mean, it's not like these people are *stupid*, you

know? Everyone knew what was going on—everyone except my dad, I guess—so it's not like these fucking reporters actually thought that these videos had anything to do with reality. It's just like, this little fucking game we're all supposed to play. EVERYONE involved in the process knows it's bullshit, like, every single person knows EXACTLY what's going on, but we all still have to pretend like it's real. They all have to pretend like they're ACTU-ALLY curious about what my answers are gonna be to these questions, and I have to pretend like I don't know for a fact that they're lying. And half of the time, I just want to be like: Can we drop it for a second? Can we just, like, take the day off? But Content Bucket was absolutely loving it, you know, because these were some of their most popular videos ever, and they were driving a lot of traffic to their site, and meanwhile, like, I'm trying to get in con-tact with them—I'm sending them all these emails being like: Hey, listen, my dad is obviously sick. Why don't you just tell me how to get in contact with him so I can get him some help?—but they were like: Your father doesn't want us to give you that information. We have to respect that. And I was just like: Fuck *these* motherfuckers. You know? Like, how fucking lost and empty do you have to be to become one of *these* motherfuckers? I'll never for-give those Content Bucket guys. Seriously.

And so at a certain point, I just totally disengaged. I started saying to people, like: Believe whatever the fuck you want to believe, because I've got bigger fish to fry. If I paid attention to every crazy thing that was said about me, if I responded to every crazy conspiracy theory, I'd never have time to live my life, like, I'd never have time to actually make any music, and that's what I'm supposed to be here for in the first place, right?

And so I just helped my mom and Bob with the wedding, and like, that was beautiful and it went great, and then I just disappeared for a little while to the South of France.

I just wanted to get the fuck out for a bit, you know? So I packed up and left the country and just tried to focus in. I just tried to get back into the root of the thing, which like, has always been the music—it's always just been me alone at the piano or at the computer, and like, that's what I wanted to get back to—so I found this little place that I could rent indefinitely, and the place had a grand piano, and so I was like: Dope.

And it was actually in that place in France that I started to make the album that would eventually become *Roses and Mud*. I wanted to go super-minimal, you know? Like, just me and the piano. And I actually got into a really nice groove with it when I was making those songs. I'd get up every day, and I'd have a little bit of breakfast—maybe a bowl of cereal or something—and then I'd just sit down at the piano and work for, like, hours at a time. And in the afternoons, I'd go out, like, go for a swim or some shit, and like, I'd invite different people up to come stay in the house and work on some shit with me—Scaggs dropped in, and Deez and Trick, and I even got Billy Maze to come out and sing some melodies for "Pump Bottle"—and it was this really dope setup. I just wanted to basically stay there for like, a couple of months, even a year, because back home all the shit with my dad and all the rumors and all that shit were just getting way too intense, and so I just didn't even wanna be there at all. I was considering for a moment just like, totally uprooting my life and moving to France for good, but then, you know, the only reason I decided to even go back was because my mom was having the baby, and I obviously wasn't gonna miss that.

I was surprised at first when she told me that she and Bob were expecting, but you gotta remember, my mom was super-young when she had me—she was only, like, twenty years old or something—and so it actually wasn't that crazy, biologically, for her to give it another go. Plus, you know, Bob is estranged from his son—the kid he had however many years ago with his ex-wife—and so I think he was really into the idea of creating a whole new family with my mom and me.

I've actually never told anybody about this, but my dad reached out to me a few days before he died. I had been trying to contact him for a while to get him to stop making those videos, and then I just sort of peaced out on him and peaced out on the country, but three or four days before he died—you know, like, three or four days before I got on the flight back to L.A. to see my mom and Bob—I got this crazy message from him in my in-box. I didn't really think much of it at the time, because, like, he didn't even say anything on it, but I guess it must've been some sort of cry for help, or like, maybe even some kind of suicide note, because he didn't leave anything behind when he shot himself. Looking back on it now, I guess this message he left in my in-box was like, his version of saying good-bye or his version of saying fuck you, and it was crazy, because, like, it's not even like he called

JUSTIN KURITZKES

me on the phone and tried to actually *talk to me*. Like, he didn't want me to actually be able to respond to him. He just like, recorded something on his phone and emailed it to me from his official Content Bucket email address, and I was supposed to open it up and sit with it and figure out what the fuck to do with it for the rest of my life. And all it was was this very dark, very grungy acoustic guitar cover of that first song I wrote with Deez—the one that sort of started all this shit—with my dad singing the main lyrics. It was literally just my dad and his guitar, and he played through the whole song. And I didn't respond to it or anything because at the time, I was just sort of like: What the fuck is this? But I have to say, like, the way he was singing that song was actually kind of next-level. I mean, literally no one's ever heard it before—I haven't even told my mom about it—but like, it was kind of the best work my dad had done in years. Maybe if I ever release that covers album of the stuff we recorded back at the radio station in St. James, I'll include this thing my dad sent me as like, the last track, because I think it would really freak people out, you know? Like, how deep of a move would that be? To just drop that shit at the end?

But, you know, it was really fucked up of my dad to do it when he did it, because literally three days after he died, my mom gave birth to Lenny, and so Lenny's birth was overshadowed by all this horrible darkness. Here was this day that was supposed to be all about joy—you know, my mom's joy and Bob's joy and just generally, like, the *joy of life*—and instead it became all about anger and resentment and death. I was coming out of the hospital, going down the street to go pick up coffee for my mom and Bob, and like, the reporters outside were just asking me about my dad's suicide, and it's like: Guys, I'm at the hospital to watch my MOM give BIRTH to my BROTHER, you know? Even when I was literally, like, wheeling my mom out of the hospital with Bob and the baby, people are shouting shit at my mom and me about my dad, and I was just like: GUYS! Time out! Please!

But, you know, the irony is my dad was always sort of a PR genius. It's crazy how creative people can get when they don't give a fuck anymore. That's something I think about a lot, like, when I'm creating, is just like: How can I create like I don't give a fuck? How can I create like there's nothing left to lose even though, like, I've got *so much* to lose, you know? Because there's a lot of freedom in that. There's a whole world of potential that gets opened up when you decide to create from a place of just total not caring.

Because, you know, that was my dad's problem, right, is that it all started to mean too much to him. Like, he was just taking life so seriously. But the moment he decided he was going to kill himself, like, the moment he decided it didn't even matter to him anymore, all of a sudden, all of this creative energy started to brew up in him, and he was able to have, like, some actually exciting ideas. Like, that sort of grungy cover he sent me was actually sort of dope. If he had proposed THAT for the next album instead of the shit he had shown me, maybe we would've never had any of the problems we had in the first place, because it would've just been like: Whoa, Dad, amazing. And the way he timed the suicide, I mean, what a work of art, you know? What perfect execution.

But I guess that's the thing about suicide is that it's never a particularly creative thing to do so much as it just shows a certain level of *commitment*. Like, what's exciting about suicide, from an artistic point of view, isn't so much that it's so amazingly smart or so amazingly original, but it's more just like: I can't believe he *went* there, you know? Like, when those monks set themselves on fire, it's not like that's the most amazing idea in the world—it's not as if my mind is blown that anybody thought of that—because, like, at the root of it, it's actually kind of a deeply stupid thing to do. Like, the easiest thing in the world to do is to just blow your brains out or to set yourself on fire, but the fact that someone actually DID it, like, the depth of the commitment it takes to actually follow through on such a stupid idea, is actually kind of breathtaking, because it's like: That's the *last* thing you ever get to do. Like, for my grandpa, the last thing *he* got to do was crap his pants and fall asleep. And he probably didn't even *know* that it was the last thing he was ever gonna do. He just did it and dozed off thinking, like: Gonna wake up again tomorrow and be in more pain and crap my pants some more! And then he just never woke up. But my dad like, got a fucking shotgun and loaded it up with shells, and, fully conscious of what he was doing, like, put the barrel in his mouth and put his finger on the trigger and blew his fucking brains out.

He did it in the house I grew up in. LOL. I guess I forgot to mention that. Probably most of you already knew that, but it turned out that's where my dad had been staying this whole time: the last place I ever would've thought to look. He was just renting out our old house in St. James, making all those crazy videos for Content Bucket in front of a green screen in the basement, and like, sleeping in the room he used to share with my mom. And the day he decided to kill himself, he went up to the room that used to be my room, you know, the room where we recorded that video of me singing the national anthem, and he sat at the little desk that used to be my desk, and he leaned the gun up against the desk, and he leaned his head onto the gun, and he pulled the trigger. And like, the only reason he did it that day instead of some other day that week was that he knew the housekeeper was gonna come by that day, and so he knew someone would find him and report it and we'd all hear about it on time. I mean, it's like I said, you know, there's nothing particularly remarkable about killing yourself that way. There's nothing particularly original or creative or interesting about it, but it's just, like, the FACT that he did it is so powerful, you know? There's some real sense in which, like, you just can't *top* that. You can't top, like, my dad sitting at my desk in the house I grew up in, literally blowing his brains out all over the room. That's the best he's ever gonna do. That's the best anyone could ever possibly do. Which is why I think, like, for so many artists who can't create anymore, it just makes so much sense to choose suicide as the next move, because it's like, the most complete work of art we're capable of. I mean, what could be more meaningful? What could be more powerful than just removing yourself from the equation? It's the only power we ALL fucking have, but by doing it you're just going, like: Yeah, I pushed the fucking button. In a way, it's like you're ending the whole fucking world, because, as far as you're concerned, once you're gone, there's nothing left. And what better artistic state-ment could there be? What more intense thing could you do than just end the whole fucking world for yourself?

LOL.

Here's something I learned recently:

The only reason tattoos stay in our skin for so long is that our body thinks it's under attack.

Did you know that?

I'd been getting tats for years before finally I asked my main guy—this dude Optimus Prime who's got a shop on Melrose—like: Yo, how does this shit even work? And what he told me was that tattoos are basically little infections.

When the needle pierces our skin and injects ink into the lower level—like, not just the surface level but the layer that's way beneath that—our body freaks out, and it's like: What the fuck is happening to me? And so it sends all of these immune cells to the places where the needle is attacking it, and when the cells try to fight off the ink, they eat up all the dye and soak it up into the skin. And most of the particles in the ink get eaten up by the cells no problem, but the pigment cells—the cells that have all the color—are too big to get broken down, and so they just stay there, trapped in the skin forever. And you're always shedding layers of skin, so like, eventually they DO fade, but for most tats to disappear completely, you'd basically have to live, like, *three hundred years* or some-thing, and so for all intents and purposes, they're perma-nent.

Which makes you think, like: What makes a perfect tattoo?

Or, I mean, I guess I'm not really concerned with what makes a *perfect* tattoo, because like: What the fuck does *that* even mean? But I do ask myself all the time, like, WHY should I get this tat or like, why should I get that tat? And it always ultimately boils down to: How badly do I want it? How much do I believe in this thing?

Because, you know, once you get started, it's really hard to stop. I mean, once you realize that the pain isn't that bad, and once you get over the initial nervousness about, like, it being forever, it's really easy to just go way the fuck overboard and tat your whole body up. Like, Z Bunny for instance, or Skelet0r: Those dudes just LOVE getting tattoos. And for Z at least there's no decision-making process at all. If it occurs to him one minute that maybe he should get a tat, he'll get it. The second he gets that feeling of like, *Hmm, that'd be cool*, it's already pretty much inked on his body. All he needs to do is go to the parlor and sit in the chair. And I've literally been with him countless times where we'll just be watching a movie or whatever, or like, driving down the street, and he'll just point to something and be like: Shit, whoa, I gotta get that on my leg. Or like: Bro, watchu think? Should I get that on my forehead? And sometimes it's just the stupid-est shit, you know? Like, no disrespect at all to Z—that guy's my boy for life—but like, motherfucker has a tattoo of a Snickers bar on his nose because one day he was eat-ing one, and he was just like: This might be my favorite candy . . . and two hours later, like, legitimately no joke, we're at the tattoo parlor and I'm going: Yo, Z, you sure about this, man? And Z is just laughing like: What kind of *question* is that?

So that's one attitude that you can have. And that's cool. I mean, I respect that. But I find myself being a little more selective when it comes to the shit I put in my skin. I mean, I have a TON of tats, don't get me wrong. Like, compared to most people you'd see in a coffee shop or like, on the beach or whatever, I'm a dude with a *lot* of tats, that's just part of my identity, but for someone like Z or for someone like Skelet0r, it's just like, EVERY fucking inch of their bodies is *covered*, you know? You can barely see the skin.

And I think, for me, like, there are a few main things I like to consider before I get anything tatted on me, and those are:

#1. Aesthetic—I don't want to put something on my skin that just looks lame.

#2. Meaning—I want every tattoo to mean something to me on at least two or three levels. Ideally, four.

And #3. Staying Power—Will I still be happy looking at this thing when I'm eighty? Will this mean anything to me in the nursing home?

That last one is kind of the trickiest, you know, because you have to make a prediction about where your mind's gonna be at in the future, and I don't really think anybody is particularly good at that. I mean, for someone like Z or for someone like Skelet0r, they're both just sort of like: Whatever. The only thing that's real to me is right now, and right now I want a fucking Snickers bar on my nose. And I totally respect that. I actually think that's kind of a dope way to live. But I try to think about my own tattoos from the perspective of my whole life, because, like, I don't know, I care about that guy in the future. I want him to have a good time.

Like, for instance, I don't have any tattoos about my dad—at least not directly—because I'm still not sure how that's gonna sit over the years. Like, I've got a ton of stuff about my mom—I've got a rabbit, which is her favorite animal, and a dentist's chair to commemorate all those years she was working—but I don't really have anything to do with my dad, because, like, I don't really know if I want to see that shit every day, you know? Like, if I got the dates of his life or like, his name and "RIP" or something, I'm just not sure I want to be reminded of that shit every time I look in the mirror, or like, every time I get out of the pool.

Because one of the beautiful things about tattoos, one of the things I really love about them, is that you forget about them sometimes—like, especially when you have as many as I do, you forget about certain ones for days, weeks at a time—and then you'll be reminded of them sort of randomly throughout the day or throughout the year, because, like, one of them catches your eye or like, someone will ask you about it when they see you with your shirt off or your pants off, and you'll be like: Oh, right, that thing! And if you've chosen your tattoos well—like, if you've only put stuff on your body that you really care about—those moments are actually sort of beautiful, because you get to talk about something that's really special to you, and you get to let this other person a little bit deeper into your world. But I just don't know that I want to set myself up to be ambushed every once in a while by these memories of my dad and all the shit he put us through, because I'm not sure how I'm going to react to that. I'm not sure it would be a good idea to plant a little land mine like that on my body.

I'm only thinking about all this shit because a few weeks ago, I had my assistant commission this graphic designer to draw up that diagram I was talking about of all my tats, and she just finished it and sent it over to me a few minutes ago, and I've been sitting here on the plane looking at it, like: Wow. There are so many talented people in the world. She really knocked it out of the park.

It was kinda funny, because, like, in order to make sure the diagram was accurate, I had to let my assistant take pictures of every inch of my body. I mean, some of the tattoos are really small, so I wanted the diagram to have all these blown-up sections, you know, like a biology textbook or something, where we zero in on just one little patch and like, get a super-close-up view of all the various tats there, and so we spent like, an hour or two in my living room a few weeks back with me just like, completely naked and her circling around me with a camera. I don't even think she knew about all of them, you know? Like, usually I show her every new tat when I get one—I'll send her a pic from the parlor or whatever while the ink is still settling in—but a few times during the photo shoot, she was just like: Whoa, really? And I was like: Yeah, you didn't know about that one?

I think the one that surprised her most was this little devil guy I have tattooed in between my big toe and my pointer toe on my right foot. It's just this super-terrifying demon guy that I got in Indonesia when we were stopped over there with the *HERE we Go* tour. One of our technicians had this absolutely terrifying, like, traditional devil mask tattooed on his neck, and I was just like: Oh my god, that's the dopest thing I've ever seen. And he was like: Oh, thanks, my friend did it. And I was like: Do you think he could do one for me? And the guy was like: Of course! Let me call him up. And the tattoo artist was super-excited to do it. I mean, he was a fan, and he was super-talented, and I was just like: I want it in my toes. I want to crush the devil with my toes. And he was like: Okay, cool, but I'm just warning you: That's gonna hurt *a lot*. And I was like: Whatever, man, let's fucking roll. And it REALLY fucking hurt. LOL. The whole time during the show the next day, I was like, limping around the stage and shit, trying to hold it together.

On the diagram, there's two main images of me just standing there with my arms out—there's a front view and a back view—and then there's all these smaller sections, and it's like, the graphic designer got every inch. She didn't miss anything. It's actually really fucking beautiful, you know, to see yourself like that—to see yourself so fully rendered. I'll include the whole thing in the final version when they publish it and it'll be like one of those glossy sections, you know, with a key and everything—like, when you pick up the book, you'll see that there's just this section in the middle with this different-colored, different-textured paper, and then when you finally get to it, you'll be like: Whoa! Cool!—but for now, I'll just write down the little descriptions every once in a while whenever I have the time. She already labeled all the tattoos with numbers and everything on the diagram, so all I have to do is write down the descriptions and the little stories that go along with each of them. It's WAY too much work to do it all in one go—if I tried to do it right now, it'd take me, like, five hours at a minimum—so I'll have to just chip away at it gradually.

The dudes are all passed out—we're just finishing up this sort of insane leg of the tour where we went all through Central Europe, you know, like Prague, Berlin, Budapest, Vienna—and now we're heading home. On the way there, I decided I wanted to stop over in Svalbard and finally visit my man Oddvar at the seed vault to see what that's all about.

LOL.

He's been telling me for a while that I should drop by. I've always wanted to check it out and hang with Oddvar on his home turf, but I've been too busy with one thing or another, and so it never ends up happening, but then, finally, two weeks ago, Oddvar emailed me telling me that he's naming a seed after me, so I was like okay, all right, I should probably go visit him.

Apparently, there are some seeds that they catalog over there that don't have names yet because like, there are some plants that I guess people are discovering every once in a while for the first time or like, cataloging for the first time, and so this plant—I guess it's a kind of shrub that's found in New Zealand?—they didn't have an official name for it yet—it just had like, a number—and so Oddvar decided that he was going to name it after me.

Which is dope, you know, because, like, imagine a thousand years from now, something horrible happens and the whole world ends and they have to rebuild every-thing from scratch and they're just like, shit, we need to plant some *shrubs*, you know, and so they dig into the vault and pull out this seed that's got my name on it and they're like, okay, no idea who this guy is, but this looks okay. And then, like, all over the world, people are running through fields of shrubs with my name or like, losing their volleyballs in my shrubs and having to go in there to find them. I don't know. Something about that just really makes me happy.

After Oddvar sent me that email, I wrote him back asking him if he'd read some of the pages I had written so far, because like, I'm actually kind of curious to hear what he thinks of the book, and I was like: Yo, Oddvar, I need you to keep this totally confidential, and you can't show this to anyone, but I need someone to take a look at these pages I've been writing and tell me if they feel hon-est, you know? Tell me if they sound like me. And Odd-var wrote me back immediately being like: I would be honored to take a look. I'll write you some thoughts at the end of the week. So that was pretty cool of him.

I like Oddvar. I don't think Oddvar really *cares* if I like him, and like, I'm not even sure he *likes me*, you know—like, I don't think that's a part of his whole relationship to me—but I think we could actually be really good friends if we lived in the same place or kept up more of a correspondence.

He wrote me back a few days ago with like, all these super-thoughtful notes about the book—like pages and pages of thoughts—and I was reading through all of it, you know, just like, this mountain of thoughtfulness, and

I was like: Okay, I can't write a fucking email back to this guy. I have to go see him and talk about this shit in person. So I wrote him back being like: Oddvar, can I stop by the seed vault on Thursday? I'm gonna be flying back home from Europe. And he was just like: Of course, yes. I'll have a room made up for you and your entourage. LOL. He actually said "entourage."

Patrick's not happy about it. I mean, I get it, you know, he's the head of my security detail, and like, yeah, Oddvar's super-chill, but at the end of the day, like, he's still a FAN, you know, and fans should always be treated with suspicion. Plus, we probably won't even be getting cell service on this fucking island, so Patrick's just like: There's too many variables to control. I strongly advise against it. But I was just like: You know, Patrick, I respect that, and like, you know I love you and I respect one hundred percent what you do for me, but at the end of the day, this is what I want to do, and this is my decision, so this is what we're doing.

And I mean, whatever, by the time we get there, he's gonna love it. All the guys will. I can already picture it: like, Patrick and Curt and Mo just throwing snowballs at each other on the ice, and drinking beer out in the snow and looking off into this endless expanse of nothing and just being like: Wow, guys, we're at the end of the world. We're in some James Bond shit. Their inner Viking will take over.

Apparently, tourists aren't allowed into the Vault. There's a lot of people every year who head up to Svalbard to catch the northern lights, because, like, it sounds like they're really beautiful from there, and the tourists are always asking the guides like: Yo, can you take us to the Vault? Can we go check out the Vault? But Oddvar was telling me that your average person isn't allowed to just waltz in and look around. You need to be somehow associated with the people who work there, or like, you need to be an invited guest.

Something I also didn't realize is like: This isn't the only seed vault in the world. Apparently, there a couple thousand of these things that have been set up by different organizations all over the place, and this one is just what they call the "Doomsday Vault": It backs up the whole system. EVERY seed that you can find at one of those other vaults, like, every single one, you can find a duplicate here. Like, there's a seed vault in Italy that only has different kinds of tomatoes and basil and whatever, and like, there's a seed vault in Lebanon that only has different kinds of Lebanese seeds. But this vault, like, the one in Svalbard, has *everything*. It has ALL the seeds from ALL the different places on Earth just in case any of those regional seed banks get wiped out.

And Oddvar was telling me that it happens all the time. Like, apparently, because of all the shit that's been going on in the Middle East, a few of the seed vaults over there have been completely destroyed. Like, they've been bombed to shit by the U.S. or fucking pillaged and burned to the ground by one of those crazy militant groups. And so the Svalbard vault has to back them up. Some of those plants are so rare even that like, the Svalbard vault is the only place in the world now where they even *exist* anymore, you know? Without the Doomsday Vault, those plants would've just been gone forever—wiped off the face of the earth.

Anyway, I'm gonna try to get some shut-eye for the rest of the flight—I want to be totally fresh and rested for when we get there—but before I close my eyes, I just wanted to catalogue this one tat on the diagram before I forget: the first tat I got after my dad died. I was just reminded of it because of all the shit I was talking about earlier.

I was obviously super-conscious of the fact that like, whatever I got at that point was gonna be majorly significant, you know? Like, the timing just made it so that whatever I ended up getting was gonna have a lot of *heaviness* attached to it, a lot of weight, and so I wanted to do everything I could to counteract that. Like, I knew that the worst thing I could do would be to wait, like, a couple months or whatever until I found the "right thing" to put on my body, and so literally a week after he died, like, only a few days after we put him in the ground, I just went to see Optimus, and I was like: Yo, what's a tat that I'm always talking about getting but that we haven't gotten around to? And Optimus thought for a second, and he was like: What about the map of St. James? And I was like: Dope. Perfect. And then he tatted it on the back of my left thigh.

It's #63 on the diagram.

The funeral was pretty low-key.

There weren't that many people there. I mean, you know, there were a few people who felt like they had to come—people who had been working for me for a while like my road manager, Bobby, and my manager, Shari, and some of the record label guys—but at that point, there weren't that many people left who actually gave a shit about my dad or his life. A few of his band mates from the early days were there—guys like Greg and Daniel and Harry who were all part of the grunge scene in St. James—but that was pretty much it in terms of "friends." His dad, my grandpa, was already dead, and his mom was already in a nursing home.

Honestly, there were more paparazzi than guests, so the whole thing had this very weird vibe around it. It felt like everybody who was actually there to bury my dad was doing some sort of performance art piece and the cameras were just there to document it. Like, obviously, the photographers had to keep a certain distance, but we could still hear the cameras clicking from over the fence, and every once in a while, we'd see the flash, so it really felt like we were actors on a film shoot and the paparazzi were the crew.

It's ridiculous, because like, obviously, there are a ton of different cemeteries in L.A. where the view is completely blocked off from the public, but my dad specifically said in his will that he wanted to be buried at this one particular place where like, there's a clear view from the street. And, I mean, honestly, it's insane that he even wanted to be buried in L.A. in the first place, because you have no idea how much it costs to have a body transported that far—especially one with its head blown off. I mean, *I could afford it*, I'm not complaining, but it still just felt like a dick move.

Mandy came with me. Mandy's mom too. We all hung

out a lot when Mandy and I were coming up in the scene together, so I guess they both wanted to pay their respects. Kelly is actually a really dope person. I'm not sure if she'll read this, but if she does, I hope she knows how much I love and respect her. She's the best.

Of course, everybody saw Mandy and me standing next to each other in the photos, and they were immediately like: Are the two of you back together? For a couple weeks after the funeral, there was all this speculation about whether the two of us had started things up again, and the truth is she was really just there as my friend. I just really needed her.

My mom and Bob didn't come to the funeral. I'm sure my dad would've wanted them to, but my mom just had a newborn baby, and she wasn't about to get a sitter. Plus, you know, she *definitely* wasn't going to bring the baby with her to the funeral. She knew, even before it happened, *exactly* what kind of event it was going to be—my dad literally couldn't surprise her at this point—so I honestly just don't think she could stand to be a part of it anymore.

Sometimes, when I think about my mom's life, I just think about it as this thing that's been completely defined by men. Like, whether it's my dad or Bob or me, my mom is always getting caught up in some dude's life, like, being defined in relationship to some man she loves. And sometimes, it feels like all she does is just answer for her men and apologize for us and deal with the consequences of our actions. Which is why I'm really stoked that she's got her jewelry line now, because like, that's something *she* actually really cares about for herself. I think it's really allowed her to shine in a way that she hasn't been able to before. I mean, she's always been making jewelry—like, even back when she was a dental assistant, she would be tinkering around with beads in the living room at night or making little Christmas presents for my aunts and my cousins—but now, like, she's able to do it on a bigger scale with some nicer materials, and so her creativity has just been able to flow. Bob's been so supportive of it too, which is dope. He doesn't just sort of go like: Oh wow, that's amazing! Good work, honey! He actually critiques it and helps her out with business concepts and talks through the ideas with her. That's what I mean when I say people don't know Bob. He's such a sweetie when it comes down to it. I wish people could see that.

My mom made me this little cross necklace that I've been wearing to shows and on the road recently. I've just found it really comforting, you know, having a little piece of her with me. It's weird, because like, I'm not even that religious anymore—like, I don't even really think about God at all that much—but ever since I've been wearing the cross, people have been writing articles about how I'm finding Jesus again, and it's like: No, I just love my mom's jewelry. But whatever, you know, there are worse things people could be saying about me.

Weirdly, the funeral service was *uber-religious*, which was crazy because, like, out of the three of us, my dad was the one who NEVER gave a shit about religion—like, the only reason he even wanted us to keep going to church was so that I could practice my singing—but the priest at the funeral read a TON of Bible verses. We were standing out there for what had to have been an hour, just going through all this scripture. And I don't know, maybe it was just because my dad knew the speeches were gonna be short, and so he wanted to stretch the run time of the funeral for as long as he could just so that the press could get all the coverage they needed, but a part of me thinks that he really *was* a little more religious than he let on, or like, maybe God started to mean a lot to him in his final days. I don't know. It was nice to hear some of those verses again, and like, sing some of those songs. A lot of that stuff had sort of dropped out of my life, so to be reminded of it all at a moment like that was actually kind of powerful.

The choir director from St. James was there, by the way. I guess I forgot to mention that. He flew all the way out from Minnesota, and I let him crash in my guest-house for a few days. He was really heartbroken by the whole thing—I mean, everyone back in St. James was—because, you know, we were sort of an important family to all those people. Even if we hadn't visited in like, for-ever, and even if we had lost touch with most of them for a couple years, my dad's death still hit the community pretty hard, because, you know, aside from me, the most notable person to ever come out of St. James was this guy *Mike Kingery* who played for the Seattle Mariners, and, like, he wasn't even *that amazing* at baseball, you know? He was just *on the team.* So people felt really invested in my family. I don't think anybody even knew my dad was back in town until he blew his brains out. At the burial, the choir director was bawling his eyes out, which was kind of a mess, since he was supposed to be leading everybody in the songs. He'd like, get through half a verse and then sob for a bit, and then we'd all have to stand there waiting for

FAMOUS PEOPLE

him to get his shit together so we could make it to the chorus.

I ended up giving a little speech. I wasn't really planning on it, but a few people started giving speeches, so I kinda figured I had to. I knew that all the microphones on the other side of the fence were gonna be able to pick up whatever I was saying, so I kind of knew that my speech wasn't gonna just be for the people gathered there—it was gonna be for the whole world—so I just said, you know, that my dad wasn't ultimately a bad guy but that he just wasn't built for this life. I said that my dad's life should be an example to everyone of what happens when you forget that life should be fun, when you start to take it all too seriously. I kinda said, like, I'm gonna choose to remember all the good moments with my dad instead of the dark ones. I'm gonna try to remember when we were making all those recordings in St. James, or like, when we first got to L.A. and we would drive around looking at all these crazy houses and taking all these stupid pictures of each other with disposable cameras. That's how I'm gonna remember my dad. It wasn't a masterpiece or anything. I was just kind of riffing off the dome.

I'll still go visit his grave every once in a while. I don't totally know why, but sometimes I'll just find myself there—whenever I'm in the neighborhood or I'm passing by—and I'll see that people have left all kinds of stuff on the headstone. The cemetery's private for the most part, but there are certain hours of the day when anyone can come take a walk through it, so sometimes I'll see that people have left, like, little goofy things on top of the grave. Most of the time, it'll be like, printed out pictures of the memes that people used to make about him or merchandise from my tour or like, stickers or something, but sometimes, it'll be little notes for me—I guess people figure it's a place I'll drop by every once in a while—so I'll read them if I have the time. Sometimes it'll be like, people expressing their condolences, which is cool, and sometimes it'll be girls trying to get that D, which is like: Seriously? *That's* what you're gonna do here? But, you know, whatever. You have to laugh. If you can't laugh at the crazy shit people do, then your life is gonna be full of a lot of sadness.

One time, I dropped by, and I saw that Mandy had left me a little note. She didn't put her name on the front of the card or anything, but I could tell when I opened it up that it was from her. Inside, it was totally blank except for this little drawing of a seagull. LOL. I don't know exactly what she was trying to communicate, but it really touched my heart, to be honest. I can't believe we didn't know what seagulls were.

#43—Left side of my torso. This just says the name "KATE" and the date that Deez and I first played at Charizard. I kind of love that this is the only tattoo I've got with a girl's name on it, because I didn't even know this girl that well. Basically, I just got caught up in the sort of amazing vibe of that night, and I ended up hooking up with her in the green room right there at Charizard, and like, I remember her being the hottest girl I've ever seen. Like, legitimately, to this day, I still think about her. It was also the first time I had ever fucked without a condom, so the next day I was freaking out and calling up Deez and being like: YO, MAN, WHAT DO I DO?? And he was just laughing his ass off, like: Bro, chill out. I'll have my doctor come over and test you. And anyway, I was fine, but I never heard from Kate again. I texted her a few times, but she just straight up never responded. And Deez and I were laughing about it a couple years ago when we were hanging out, and it was just like, the funniest thing in the world to us, because she legitimately ghosted me. Like, that doesn't happen that often. LOL. And so a few days later, I went to the parlor and got her name tatted on my torso just as a way to commemorate that time, you know? Commemorate that moment in my life. I don't know. I kind of imagine us running into each other one day and her seeing the tattoo somehow and me being like: Ummm, yeah, about that . . .

#18—Right butt cheek. This is one of the earlier tattoos I got. It's just a treble clef and a bass clef. Pretty self-explanatory. I mean, I guess on the face of it, like, this is kind of a *lame* tattoo—like, this is kind of the lamest tattoo for a musician to have—but I think that's maybe partly why I got it? Like, I don't know, sometimes it just feels really freeing to like, *lean into* the person that a lot of people think I am—like, just get the tattoo that some creepy musician bro at a bar would get—because, like: If *I* put it on my body, then no one else can brand me with it, you know? Like, no one can be like: I bet he's the kind of guy who's got a treble clef on his ass, because then I can just be like: yeah, actually, I AM. Plus, like, all those things that we think of as lame, like, all those things we make fun of people for, are actually just very sincere, like, very beautiful things. Like, we're actually just calling those things "lame" because we can feel that the person is being really embarrassingly honest about what they find beautiful or meaningful and it sort of makes us embarrassed to be confronted with it. But like, why are we embarrassed, you know? Is it because that person is stupid, or is it because we're realizing how DEAD we are and how many bullshit defenses we've built up against simple, beautiful things? And like, why WOULDN'T I get a tattoo of a treble clef and a bass clef on my ass, you know? What could be more beautiful than the fact that we came up with a whole visual system for representing SOUNDS? I mean, seriously. I don't know. That's kind of incredible to me.

#27—Left hand. This is a thorny rose growing out of a pile of shit. We haven't gotten to the *Roses and Mud* tour yet, so I won't say too much here, but let's just say: I really deserved a tattoo after that one.

The seed vault was pretty dope.

It wasn't really much to look at—it was just like, rows and rows of boxes that, like, maybe contained the future of humanity—but it was still kind of amazing to see how everything worked.

The entrance is actually pretty cool-looking—when you approach it, there's this big triangular thing jutting out from the side of the mountain with, like, this glass skylight that looks totally futuristic and amazing—but then once you get inside, the whole thing just feels like you're in a Costco or an Ikea or something.

Oddvar showed me the seeds he named after me. He

couldn't really take them out of their package—they were vacuum packed for storage—but I could see them through the plastic, and they definitely looked like seeds. LOL. I guess there's not really much more to say about that.

I was totally right about the guys having the time of their lives, by the way. We got there, and immediately, Oddvar was like: Gentlemen, there's a foosball table upstairs and there are a few snowmobiles in the garage if you would like to use them. And before he could even get the words out of his mouth, Patrick and Curt and Mo were just off to the fucking races to see who would get first dibs. They were practically clambering over each other.

Oddvar showed me around a bit and talked about some of the experiments he was working on—I didn't understand a lot of it, but I still appreciated that he was trying to explain it all to me—and then we sat down in this little office area that had a heater and a coffee machine, and we started talking about the book.

One of his big notes was about Bob.

The publishers have been telling me that I should try and distance myself as much as possible from Bob in the book—you know, they think it might hurt sales for me to be associated with him—but Oddvar had pretty much the opposite note. He was basically like: It might be interesting for people to hear about Bob from my perspective—to hear from me which parts of Bob's writings I've come to find so useful—especially since like, Bob's written a lot of shit, and people might just assume that I find it all equally meaningful because of the relationship we have.

And I guess I usually kind of avoid that stuff. Not necessarily because I don't want to talk about it—like, anyone who knows me at all will tell you: If you wanna talk about Bob Winstock, I'm game to throw down whenever—but I guess I've avoided talking about it publicly because, like, first of all, I don't want to sound like Bob's *spokesman*—like, I don't want people to mistake my interpretation of his writings for his *intention* or whatever—and second of all, like, I just don't really believe in stepping out of my lane. I'm not an academic. I'm not a public intellectual. At the end of the day, I make songs and I sing songs, and like, yeah, I'm one hundred percent all for challenging myself and expanding the scope of what I can do—I mean, that's why I'm trying to make this video game, you know, or like, even this *book*—but I'm also a firm believer in not trying to overstep my boundaries too much. Like, yeah, I like to do crazy projects every once in a while and push myself and push my limits, but I've just seen so many people—like, because they have success in one field or like, because people love them for this one thing they do—start thinking that they can do ANYTHING. Like, all of a sudden, they think that they can go around speaking at conferences and being *ambassadors* for shit that, like, people actually devote their whole *lives* to, and so they just end up looking like assholes.

But, you know, I respect Oddvar. I think he's a smart guy, and he knows me really well, and, like, unlike the fucking publishers, I believe that he's actually coming from a place of what would be best for me and best for the book, so I'll give it a shot.

I guess the first way I connected with Bob—like, the first little tidbit of his teachings that worked its way into my life—had to do with art and the creation of art and what it means to be an artist. I mean, you know, if you've made it this far in the book, you know that I think about that shit all the time, but Bob had this really interesting take on it, and talking to him about it, or like, reading his books about it made me think about what I was doing for the first time as like, not just this thing that was about *me* and my ambition and like, trying to kill it and get ahead in the game, but actually as this other thing, this more *human* thing that could actually serve some *purpose* in the world.

Honestly, one of the things that I really appreciated about Bob when we first had that dinner at the Cuban place is that he never once said the word "responsibility." He never once told me I had a *responsibility* to my fans or that, like, I had to be a *role model* for them. And I would always hear people say shit like that, and it would always kind of piss me off, because it was like: What do they even *mean*, you know? Before I met Bob, like, when I was just starting out, *I* would say that shit all the time, because I felt like I HAD to—it felt like if you *didn't* say that shit, people were going to think you were shallow or ungrateful or entitled or an asshole—but the whole time I was saying it, like, any time I found myself in an interview saying that I wanted to set a *good example* for my fans, I would just always leave the room kind of hating myself, because I could tell that I didn't mean it. It was just like this little bit of taxes I had to pay. "Gratefulness taxes." And then Bob came along, and what he taught me was that it's not about *responsibility* or being a *role model* or *giving back*. It's not about paying back some *debt* that you owe the world for putting you in the position you're in.

It's about *expanding people's minds*, demonstrating for people what *freedom* really looks like in a human form.

According to Bob, the world is organized to make us all feel unfree. That's the point of basically every structure we've built as a society—whether it's the government or the economy or our families or whatever—it's all working against us all the time to make us feel like we don't even own our own lives, like we're all slaves to some project that we didn't even sign up for. And the only people who get to feel differently, like, the only people who get to live like none of that even matters, are people like me. Not just wealthy people, you know—because there are plenty of wealthy people who buy into the bullshit just as much as anybody else, maybe even more—but basically anybody whose life doesn't fit into the given mold, anyone who has to live in a way that's completely separate from the world that's been laid out for everybody else.

In his book *The Problem with the Middle*, Bob gets into this really crazy thing about how uber-wealthy, uber-famous people and like, uber-destitute, uber-penniless people are actually really similar, because the world hasn't really been set up for *either* of them. Like, obviously if you're uber-wealthy and uber-famous, like, the world SUPPORTS that and you can live super-well, but most of society, most of what's been built up around us, most of the ads you see and most of the infrastructure that's in place and most of the rules that you're told you have to follow, like, when you get down to it, it's all geared toward the *middle* people, you know, the *normal* people. And to a really famous, really wealthy person or like, a really poor, really destitute person, none of that shit makes any sense, because it's just so obvious that it doesn't apply to us. Like, so many times, I'll be watching TV on an airplane or like, watching a movie or something, or I'll be driving around and I'll see an ad for something on the side of the highway, and I'll just be like: That has absolutely nothing to do with me! And for a really poor person, like, the exact same thing is happening, except the reason it doesn't have anything to do with them is that they can't afford it—they see an advertisement for a water park or a restaurant or something and they're just like: I couldn't ever afford to go there, so that place is barely even real to me. But for me, it's like, the reason I can't go to those places is because if I *tried*—like, if I tried to just go to a water park and get on one of the rides and like, have some chicken fingers or something—the whole park would shut down. That entire day for everybody at the park would become all about ME being there, and every single function of the park—like, every single thing that makes the park run—would just come to a screeching halt. The only way I could even *think* about going to one of those places is if I called ahead and rented out the whole park for the day, because my presence alone will just cause all this pandemonium. And I'm not just talking about me, you know? I'm not just talking about MY comfort. I'd be doing it for the sake of the *park*. Like, I'd HAVE to do it, or else I'd be a DICK, because if I just show up somewhere, like, if I just stroll into a space that's meant for normal people and I don't give everybody the proper warning, that affects people's lives whether they give a shit about me or not. And so it's just so obvious to me that the park is a space that wasn't built for me at all. It's just so obvious that they didn't consider me or people like me when they were planning it, and they didn't consider me when they were advertising it, and they're still not really considering me until the day I show up and create a problem for them. And I think a really poor person feels the same way. They just look out at so much of the world around them and think: This isn't mine. I'm actually not welcome in any of this. For all intents and purposes, we both—me and the poor person— live in separate worlds from everybody else, but we're also both in constant contact with the normal people world—the world that everybody else lives in—and so we both kind of have to navigate it and negotiate with it because it's the only thing that exists. Like, we have to burrow our own little holes within this world and build our own societies within this larger society that mostly doesn't include us just so that we can have a space to live. And like, obviously, *my* society is a lot nicer than the poor person's—I'm not COMPLAINING about my situation at all—but the thing I have in common with the really poor person is that we both have to go around the rules. We both have to get creative and create our own spaces and find our own pockets within the world that exists just so that we can live our lives. And what that does, I think, or like, what that makes possible for both of us is that we can see that the world around us, the world that most people live in, is just total bullshit. Like, the normal people world is not "reality." It's not some concrete fact of the universe. It's just a story that a lot of people are telling themselves at the same time. But the very fact that we exist—me and the really poor person— the very fact that we're breathing and eating and walking around on the same Earth as everybody else is a rejection of the idea that the way most people live is "normal" or "natural" or "necessary."

And for Bob, like, the problem with the people in the middle, the problem with normal people, is that they take the world *so seriously,* you know? They look out on the world around them and they treat it all with this heavy seriousness, because for them, there's never any reason to doubt it. It all seems like it's been perfectly arranged just for them, and so they treat anything that threatens it with this really intense *heaviness.* But what's actually required is a sort of *lightness,* you know what I'm saying? For the normal people, for the people in the middle, the world that exists is this unshakable, unmovable thing. And they may not even know it, but they're hungry for another world. The only reason they show up to my concerts, and like, the only reason they consume so much media and spend so much time obsessing over people like me and my life is that they're hungry for an image of a world where all the bullshit they tell themselves every day just isn't real. They're hungry to let go. And so when people show up to my concerts, that's the only time they're really allowing themselves to be free, because it's the only time they're allowing themselves to imagine another way of being.

That's actually why I wear all this crazy shit all the time, you know? Or at least that's part of the reason. I mean, I *like* the shit I wear, no question about it—I think it looks dope—but it's also like: I wear this shit to communicate that I'm *not from here.* I'm a different kind of human. So many people make fun of the way I dress all the time, or like, they make fun of the way Scaggs dresses or Z dresses, and it's like: Yeah, okay, whatever, have your fun, but at the end of the day, like, you NEED us to dress this way, because the main function we serve in your lives is to give you an image of another way of existing. We NEED to look different from anybody you know or like, anybody who works in your office. And it can be something as simple as like: You're not allowed to wear sweatpants to a really fancy restaurant. I hear that and I go: What if I get a REALLY fucking fancy pair of sweatpants? What if I get a pair of sweatpants that's more expensive than a three-piece suit? What then?

And I'm not saying that people are just interested in me because they want all the STUFF that I have. Like, it's honestly not about the money or the girls or the jets or the clothes or whatever. I mean, yeah, maybe it's a *little bit* about that—like maybe people are getting off a little bit on imagining having all the material shit that I have—but what Bob says, and what I really think is right, is like: When normal people see my life, when they see the way I'm existing, they can see for a moment that another world is possible. They can see, through me, a portal into all the infinite possibilities of the human species. And so when they come to my shows or when they watch my videos, they're not actually fantasizing about being ME. They're fantasizing about being FREE.

And for Bob, like, the worst thing you can do as an artist is to try to hold on to your normal person status. Like, you can't just think of yourself as a normal person who got really lucky or who gets to do a really cool job, because when you do that, you're totally backing away from the actually amazing thing about doing what we do.

He especially thinks it's stupid to try to make art that's *soothing* for normal people or that makes them feel better or gives them a break, because, for Bob, like, they're barely ALIVE, you know? There's nothing about these people's lives that's worthy of any sort of reward or congratulations or pat on the back. And he doesn't mean that they're *bad people* or something—I mean, I know it sounds like he *hates* them or like he *looks down on them* or something—but actually, when you think about it, like, Bob is being super-*loving* toward normal people, because he's just trying to be honest with them. He loves them enough to see them clearly. How many people are willing to do that?

But, you know, people don't really want to hear about that shit. People hear me say that or they hear Bob say that, and they think I'm judging them or they think Bob's judging them, and it's like: No, I'm not judging you. I just want people to be honest. I just want people to look at their lives and go: Whoa. Shit. But that's hard, you know, because when people are honest with themselves, most of the time, the thing they have to be honest about is that they're really fucking miserable, and so it makes sense to me that they might just want to forget everything and turn their brains off for a few hours and dance.

It's like I said: You can't control what people do with your shit. If you tried, you'd go crazy. Part of my freedom—part of what makes me free—is that I can just make the music and play the shows and then let the chips fall where they may. I'm not a priest, you know? I'm not a missionary. Maybe none of this shit even matters anyway, so like, why would I get so wrapped up in it? We're all just little turds who are floating through time for a brief moment until one day we're not, and so sometimes, the only rational thing to do is to just chill out and eat a hamburger. That's what Bob taught me more than anything: You've gotta be able to take life more seriously than anyone else and less seriously than anyone else, and if you can't switch back and forth between the two—like, if you can't transition at the drop of a hat—you're not nearly as free as you think you are. And along the way, you might piss some people off, or you might lose some people, but that's just part of the journey.

That was always the biggest tension between Bob and Mandy. One minute Bob would be saying the most serious thing, and the next minute Bob would be saying the most ridiculous thing, and Mandy would always just be like: Which one is it? Which person are you? And Bob would be like: Both! Both! But Mandy always thought that he was fucking with her. And I get it, you know, because when Bob would talk about music or when Bob would talk about art, it would always just feel like he was talking directly to Mandy. It would always feel like a rejection of everything she stood for and everything she was about, because for Mandy, she just wanted people to have a good time and relax and take a load off at her concerts and be happy, you know? Like, most people have a lot of shit they've got to deal with, and maybe it's a little arrogant or a little judgmental to think that you know better than they do what they need at the end of the week. Mandy always just felt like Bob's position was kind of superior and a little fucked up, because like, I mean especially for her, you know, she grew up in this super-working-class family and like, her parents worked really hard so that she could take singing lessons and dancing lessons and record a demo and move out to L.A., and Mandy really kind of hated it when Bob would say that those people didn't deserve to be comforted at all or didn't deserve to be rewarded at all for all their hard work, and like, she REALLY fucking hated it when he said that they were *barely even alive,* because like, who the fuck was *Bob,* you know? To Mandy, Bob was just this rich kid aristocrat who was born into a lot of money and had the privilege of spending all his time, like, looking out on the world and going: HMMM, what do I THINK about this? And she's totally right, by the way. Bob's family was SUPER-rich. LOL. Like, even though he talks all the time about how they were the deadest people of all, like, the least free people of all, and even though he's totally estranged from them now, like, Mandy's still right to say that they totally shaped him and that there are some things about her life and her perspective that someone like Bob—no matter how smart he is or how many books he's read—could never possibly understand. And I mean, the sad thing is, you know, that Bob was only even talking about all this shit to Mandy in the first place because he really believed in her. I mean, Bob legitimately thought that Mandy was one of the most talented people in the game. He would always tease me about how much better she was than me. And he cared about her a lot because she meant a lot to me. And she did, you know? She does. She still does.

• • •

We actually did end up getting together again once, but it wasn't after my dad died. It was a few months later, when that terrorist attack happened in Berlin.

I'm sure pretty much everyone reading this already knows about it, but just in case someone's picking this book up sometime way in the future—like, if you found this in a used bookstore or something on Mars—there was a big terrorist attack at one of Mandy's concerts two years ago, and a lot of people died.

Mandy was fine, but immediately when I heard about it on the news, my heart just sank, and I was like: I've gotta go get her. I just got this feeling like: Mandy's in trouble—I've got to go be with her. And so before I even texted Mandy to see if she was okay—they reported it on the news that she wasn't hurt, so I knew that like, at the very least, she was alive—I made a call to my pilot, and I was just like: How soon do you think we could take off and get to Berlin? And he started making all the arrangements.

I was in London at the time for the opening of this musical my boy Bryan Rogers did, so it didn't take long at all to get there. I called Mandy from the plane, and she was really shaken up—I mean, I'd never heard her like that before—and I was just like: Yo, hang tight, I'm coming to get you. And immediately when we landed, I just booked it right for her hotel.

Her people had sort of rushed her away from the scene and gotten her in a car away from the venue as quickly as they could—they weren't sure whether more shit was about to go down, you know, or if like, the whole thing was about to explode, so they were just like, in full war zone mode, putting all their training to use. Thank God Mandy had such a good security team, because as soon as they realized that shots were happening, her team basically rushed onto the stage and tackled her. Mandy didn't even really know what was happening, you know, because the music was so loud, and she was in the middle of singing "Ray of Sunshine," so she was just about to hit that high note at the end of the bridge when her security people jumped onstage and rushed her off to the side. One of her guys even got hit in the process. He didn't realize it until they had already gotten her off into the backstage area and somebody was like, "Mandy, there's blood all over you!" and everyone was in a real panic for a second until they realized that it was actually Terry who was bleeding from his arm. He hadn't even looked, and then, like, he saw it and he fainted and they rushed him to the hospital. He ended up being fine.

Anyway, when I got there, Mandy was sort of surrounded by this whole group of people—her road manager and her backup dancers, and this doctor who they had called to the hotel just to make sure that she wasn't suffering from shock or anything—and I stepped into the room and saw all of the pandemonium that was happening around her, and I was just like: Yo, do you think we could maybe clear the room for a minute? I think Mandy's a little overwhelmed. And everyone was sort of like: Yeah, okay, yeah. And they shuffled out of there.

And, immediately, when everybody left, Mandy just started bawling. Like, I think in the hubbub of the whole thing, Mandy was just like, too shocked, or too shaken up to really have any emotion about it—when I called her from the plane, she sounded terrible, but there wasn't any *feeling* in it, you know? It was just so scattered, so dazed— but then once everybody left the room and she saw me, it was just like the whole dam burst open and she was sobbing, like wailing on the floor. I went over to her and held her and it was like she was shaking, you know? She was like a little hamster.

And the thing that was really disturbing to her, or like, the thing that she really couldn't stop thinking about was that like, because she didn't know what was happening—like, because it took a while for her people to realize that an attack had broken out—she was still *singing* as people were getting shot. Like, the attack had already been under way for a couple seconds, maybe even half a minute, before her team got up on the stage and covered her, and "Ray of Sunshine" has all these pyrotechnics and complicated dance moves and all this other shit, and so Mandy wasn't really paying attention to what was going on in the audience while she was performing it—she just had too much shit to do. She was in the middle of doing the song just like she would do it at any other concert when all this horrible shit was happening out in the crowd, and, I don't know, I think that's what disturbed her so much: that, like, she could be so close to all this horrible stuff and not have a clue—or that like, in the moment, she could be so wrong about the reality of the space she was in. Not to mention, like, I think it was really kind of sickening to her that while all this shit was happening, she was providing a *soundtrack* for it, you know? Like, she was providing a live soundtrack to all these horrible murders, and "Ray of Sunshine" is just this very light, very fun and breezy and meaningless sort of thing, and so the whole thing just felt kind of demented to her. She even told me that a bunch of different people had already posted videos online of the moments leading up to the attack, and she couldn't stop watching them. Like, she couldn't stop going online and watching these videos of her face, like, smiling, and doing a dance move, and like, singing about how some guy is like a ray of sunshine while all these people were getting murdered. And I told her, like: Okay, that needs to stop NOW. Like, that's order of business number one. You need to stop watching these videos. And number two, like, we're getting the fuck out of Germany.

Obviously, Mandy's team had decided to cancel the rest of the tour—there weren't that many dates left anyway—and so I just told her, like, let's go. You and me are gonna get as far away from all this shit as we possibly can. And so we got on my plane that night, and we left.

I ended up taking her to that same town in France where I was hiding out for a while during my dad's whole meltdown. I wasn't able to get exactly the same house I had stayed at before, but it was more or less the same area, and it was just as beautiful. I just thought it would be a good place for Mandy to get her bearings, you know? To remove herself from the scene for a second and remember that this thing was way bigger than her. Obviously, she felt really attacked by the whole thing, and she also felt really responsible for what had happened, and I just thought like, the best possible thing for Mandy at this point would be to take a step back and to realize that like, there were so many different forces at play that made what happened happen and that absolutely none of it was her fault.

Sometimes it's hard, you know, to remember that you're just this tiny little seahorse in the middle of the ocean. When you're someone like me or you're someone like Mandy, your existence just gets stretched out way beyond yourself, and for all intents and purposes, it feels like your concerts or your press packages or your music videos or your merchandise or all of the shit that people have branded with your name on it is a part of YOU—like it's actually one of your limbs, one of your appendages— and so when something like what happened in Berlin happens, I mean, it just feels like it happened inside your *stomach*, you know? Or like, it feels like someone did it with your *hand*: like a little alien crawled inside your body and made its way into your finger and forced you to pull the trigger.

So, I don't know, I think the trip was really useful for her.

We didn't leave the house that much at all. Every day, I would just have my guys go to the market and get us some bread and cheese and veggies, and like, I'd cook us all our meals—I'm actually a pretty decent cook—and sometimes I would be cooking for everybody, like, Mandy's security team and my security team and the two of us, but most of the time, it was just me and Mandy in the house, and so everybody else would do their own thing.

I remember one night, it was raining outside pretty hard, and so Mandy and I made a little fire and like, I made us some hot chocolate, and we just sat on the rug in front of the fireplace and imagined what our lives would have been like if we were normal people.

LOL.

We tried to imagine what would've happened to us if somehow we never got famous.

Mandy sort of imagined that she'd end up being a high school teacher—since that's what her mom was doing, and she always really admired that—and I sort of imagined that I would've gone to college and become a doctor or something, since, like, when I was still in school, I would hear all these stories about the older kids getting to dissect a pig or a frog or something like that in junior high, and I was actually kind of pissed that I never got to do it.

And we tried to imagine if we ever would've met each other in the normal people world—like, what would've had to happen so that Mandy and me would've met naturally, like, as just two people—and the scenario we came up with was, like: Mandy probably wasn't gonna leave Arizona, you know, because her whole family was there and that's probably where she would've wanted to teach, but like, when you're a doctor, you sometimes just have to do your residency basically wherever they tell you to do it, and so maybe I would've been assigned to the hospital at the University of Arizona, and like, maybe Mandy would've been there getting her teacher's degree, and then maybe we would've met in the cafeteria one day when we both reached for the same cup of pudding.

And we sort of played it out: I pretended to be this med student, and she pretended to be this teaching student, and we pretended to meet and talk about our lives, and talk about what we were studying, and I pretended to ask her out on a date.

And, you know, somewhere along the line, there was some kissing, and then there was some touching and blah blah blah, but it really wasn't about that. It was nice, you know—I mean, it's always nice with Mandy—but it felt like the whole week in France was more about us being *friends* than it was about us rekindling some big love affair. It just felt really nice taking care of each other.

And since then, you know, since being back in L.A., it's been more or less back to normal for the both of us— back to being officially "broken up." I mean, it's not like we were ever *back together,* but we sort of left it where it had been once we landed, and I think we both still feel pretty good about that. I hugged her and kissed her on the tarmac, and we both got into our different cars, and we went our separate ways. In a way, that week really reignited our friendship, you know, which had been lacking for what felt like a really long time. Or like, I don't know, I guess it *created* our friendship, since we were never really "friends" to begin with, but it's been kind of beautiful navigating this new space together. I don't really know what else to say about that.

#85—Right bicep. This is a tattoo of that little girl from "Leader's Sacrifice." You remember that video that was being passed around the internet a few years ago? She lived in one of those dictatorships—one of those places where like, the whole society is just on lockdown 24/7— and in the video, she's performing at a singing pageant they did on the official state media channel for like, the leader's birthday. And the girl had to sing this crazy song about killing anyone who criticizes the leader and torturing anyone who calls him a liar. And people were passing it around as this horrifying thing that proved how insane that society was and how unfree they all were, and like, people were writing all these messages to go along with the video like: "Look how horrible it is that they're making this adorable girl sing about these horrible things," and: "Look how horrible it is that she has to say all this shit." And I watched the video, and like, yeah, the song the girl is singing is crazy as fuck and it makes that whole society seem absolutely insane, but the main thing I was focusing on the whole time was like: This girl is really GOOD, you know? Her voice is so pure, and her diction and her pitch and her rhythm are so on point that I kind of left the video feeling like the society can't be *that* bad if it produces a voice like that. I mean, it obviously didn't make me change my opinion of that society, or like, make me start thinking that I should *move there*, but in the moments when that little girl was singing, she was a *superstar*, you know? She was in the fucking clouds. It didn't really matter what the rest of her life was like. I think the thing that actually disturbed people about the video was like: When was the last time THEY felt like that, you know? How free are most of the people THEY know compared to how free that little girl is in the moment that she's singing? How many people around them are EVER going to feel the way she feels?

#46—Back of my neck. This is a drawing Oddvar did of those shrubs from New Zealand. Right after he told me he was naming the seeds after me, I asked him to draw me a picture of what they're supposed to look like when they're fully grown, and he did it and sent it to me, and I went straight to the parlor. They don't look like anything special, but I figured if the seeds are gonna have my name, I might as well plant one on my body. And Oddvar fucking loved it when I showed it to him the other day at the seed vault. He was like: WHAT? You actually did it? And I was like: Of course, man! LOL. People have just recently started to notice this one because it's kind of small, and in a lot of the stuff that's been written up about it, they think it's a weed plant—like, they think it's a pot leaf or something—and it's like: No. I'm not gonna get a fucking weed plant tattooed on my *neck*. I mean, I know plenty of people who would—I can't even count how many pot leaves Z Bunny has—but that's just not really my vibe. Anyone who knows me at all should know that.

#72—Inner left forearm. This one's pretty self-explanatory. I've been gradually piling up my discography here since *HERE we Go* dropped five years ago. I haven't included all the EPs or the Christmas tracks or the feature spots I've done on other people's shit, because if I did that, it'd cover my whole arm, but this list is all of *my* albums so far. There's: I. *Be My Baby*, II. *HERE we Go*, III. *Roses and Mud*, and then IV. with a blank space next to it for whatever the video game's gonna be called. I don't get the ink until they've been officially released, because sometimes I change my mind about the title at the last minute, and obviously it'd be a hassle to change the tat. The "IV." is just kind of sitting there as a reminder to get to work.

. . .

I guess it's worth mentioning that, like, when it comes to *Roses and Mud*, all the shit that happened with Mandy in Berlin and France had a pretty major effect on what would eventually become the second half of the album.

In the months immediately following my father's suicide, I was kind of lost in terms of, like, what I was supposed to be doing with the album. I mean, you know, at the time that he did it, I was halfway through recording all of the stuff in France, and all of the songs I had recorded at that point were like, these super-low-key, super-delicate piano songs, and I had originally wanted to make a whole album that way, but then with my dad killing himself the way he did, the album just started making less and less sense—just going to the piano felt like an escape, you know? It felt *sentimental*—and so I was actually sort of at a loss for how to proceed. But then the shit with Mandy happened, and it was just like: Oh, okay, I think I see what this has gotta be. I mean, that's when all the *grunge* found its way onto the album, you know, and when you think about *Roses and Mud*, you think grunge, right?

This is super-dark—like, this is a kind of crazy thought—but sometimes I think my dad was trying to send me a message with his suicide. I mean, obviously he was trying to send *everyone* a message, but sometimes I think he was trying to specifically send *me* a message about the direction I needed to take my career in. A part of him must've known that something needed to HAP-PEN to me, you know? I think a part of him knew that I needed to GO THROUGH something or else, like, people were gonna be done with me. Because how long is anyone really willing to root for a kid who's been famous since he was twelve? After a while, that becomes a story that's pretty hard to relate to. And so this really dark part of me thinks that my dad almost did what he did so he could give me some *edge*, you know? Or send me off into a different direction. I mean, I don't know. This is the kind of crazy shit that being famous does to your head: A suicide isn't just a suicide. You start to think of it as just another ingredient in the story of your life, another facet of your brand.

I remember coming home from the airport after saying good-bye to Mandy, and like, sitting in my house and finally reading all the news articles about the aftermath of what had happened in Berlin—you know, like, the police manhunt, and the stories coming out about all the victims, and the sort of in-depth descriptions of the actual attacks—and, I don't know why, but something inside me was just feeling so raw and so torn up that I just wanted to listen to that recording my dad sent me a few days before he killed himself. You know how sometimes you get like that? You're just like, feeling something so intensely that you want to *lean into it*: like, you just want to sink into the bath or like, dig the knife into the wound? And so I started listening to that recording—I was just sitting there in my living room, like, listening to my dad doing this gut-wrenching version of that song I did with Deez— and, all of a sudden, it hit me. I was just like: Whoa. It flashed in front of my face like a stock ticker. And I immediately called up my guitar teacher, and I was like: Yo, we've got some work to do today. And he was like: Dope. On my way.

I mean, it's crazy that I hadn't realized that's why I chose guitar in the first place, you know? I started the lessons a week or two after my dad's funeral—honestly, I just needed something to distract me, something I could noodle around with that wasn't the album—but, all of a sudden, it became so clear why I was doing it, and it was because my subconscious mind knew way before my conscious mind did that I was recording a grunge album.

And so my teacher came over—his name's Martin. I don't know why I'm calling him my "teacher" like he's some dude who puts up flyers in Starbucks. He's this dope session musician who's played with everyone from the Pagers to the Sprinklers to the Rat Kings—and I tell him what I'm thinking, and he's like: Okay, well, let's go through some basic chord progressions. And within a week or two, I already had the skeletons of a few tracks. I mean, everyone I told about this new direction just thought I was absolutely crazy. Like, my manager was just basically like: No. And my mom and Bob were like: I don't know about this. But they all knew, you know, that once I get my mind set on something, it's pretty hard to get me off of it. And, you know, I mean, it's not like the whole thing was coming out of left field. I DID grow up with grunge—like, all those records were sitting around in my house—and when I was like five or six or seven, my dad would take me with him to all his band practices, so I would just take it all in, you know? Soak it all up. It's not totally crazy to say that grunge is my musical inheritance more than like, pop is, so when it came time to actually find my way into the songs, it was actually a lot easier than some of the stuff I had been doing before.

And the real stroke of genius—I mean, the real sort of moment when the whole project opened up for me and I realized that this wasn't just some crazy thing that popped into my head but it was actually a dope idea—was when I realized that Chris Jeffries and I had to do a collaboration.

Chris was always my dad's favorite—if my dad ever wanted to be somebody else in the world, it was Chris Jeffries. Like, seriously, when I was growing up, Chris and the Thunderbums were like, practically gods in my house, and we'd just be listening to them all the time. My dad would buy all these collector's edition recordings, and like, we'd go see them in concert whenever they came to town—they never rolled through *St. James proper*, but like, if they were playing anywhere near us, like, anywhere within a couple hours, we'd drive there—and I'm actually almost positive that like, the Thunderbums were my first concert—when I was four or five or whatever: as soon as my mom would let my dad take me.

And sitting here writing this now, I'm actually remembering this one time way early on, like, way toward the beginning of my career, when we were about to play a concert at the Staples Center in L.A., and my dad was like, looking at all the pictures of the people backstage who had performed there—you know, like, they just have all those pictures hanging up in the green room—and he stopped in front of a picture of Chris, and he was just like: Wow. Incredible. I mean, I think that's when he first realized, you know, that we had made it.

So, anyway, I started asking around to see if I knew anybody who knew Chris, and it turned out that he and Trick Hatz were members of the same country club. LOL.

I mean, that's something I find so funny about the whole industry, you know, is that like, everything is presented as if it's these totally separate categories—like when I used to go to the record store, like, especially if it was a big one, like a Virgin Megastore or a Tower Records or whatever, the different genres of music would be in totally different corners of the room. You'd have to walk like, ten minutes to get from Country to Rap. And even now, like, even on the internet, the sites are still set up to make you feel like you're entering a different world when you're looking at a different style of music—but the truth is we all know each other. We all go eat at the same restaurants, and we all send our kids to the same schools, and like, yeah, fucking Trick Hatz and Chris Jeffries are both members of the Seaside Club in Malibu.

Their kids even played on the same volleyball team, so I asked Trick if he thought he could set up a meeting between the two of us, and Trick said he'd give it a shot. I didn't want to go through the managers or whatever, because I knew Chris had been in retirement for a while, and I was pretty sure if he just got an email from some assistant or some secretary, he'd just be like: Nah, I don't think so. And so Trick mentioned it to him at one of their kids' volleyball games, and Chris was a little apprehensive at first, but I guess as a favor to Trick, he eventually agreed to meet with me.

And it was funny, you know: I guess at that time, Chris was spending pretty much ALL of his time at the

Seaside Club. Like, he had his own beach house, you know, he had his own spot to chill, but I think he just really *liked* it there. Or maybe he just liked the *ritual* of it. Like, I think he just liked getting in his car and driving down to the club and saying hi to the valet guys and going and sitting in his chair by the pool, and like, I think he mostly just liked having *somewhere to go*, you know? He had become known around town as the "Mayor of the Seaside Club" because, like, he was super-involved in all the organizational decisions, and like, all of the membership drives.

And so anyway, one day I dropped by the club at the time Trick had set up for us, and Chris was sitting there with his shirt unbuttoned by the pool, like, chilling in a pair of board shorts, sipping on a daiquiri, and when I approached him, I guess 'cause I'm so young or whatever, Chris thought I was one of the busboys, and so he was like: Oh, I'm still working on this one. And I was like: No, no, I'm not—I don't work here. I'm here to talk to you about a few things. I'm friends with Trick. And Chris was immediately laughing, like: Oh, man, I'm sorry. It was just—the way you were approaching me—it was like you were scared of me or something. Here, please, pop a squat. And so I sat down in one of the pool chairs next to him, and he ordered me a daiquiri—usually, I hate that shit, but these were legitimately next-level—and we got to talking.

And the thing you have to understand about Chris is like, he took his retirement REALLY seriously. Like, he really meant it when he was like: I'm never releasing another record for as long as I live. Because the Thunderbums, at the height of their success, were pretty legendary.

I mean, there was a time not that long ago when the Thunderbums were literally the biggest band in the world. I know it's kind of hilarious to think about that now—like, how long ago does THAT feel?—but it's still undeniably true that during their moment, during their time, they were THE band to listen to. And so Chris was really allergic to the thought of ruining his legacy by putting out new music way past his prime. He had just seen it with so many people, you know, like, people who were really at the core of their moment who stuck around too long, or like, became too desperate to stay in the game and ended up becoming jokes in the process. And the way Chris looked at it, he was like an athlete, you know? If he couldn't win the championship, he didn't want to be on the field.

And so even though he wasn't that old at all—I mean, he's only like, a little bit older than my parents, so . . . late forties? Early fifties?—even though he still had a lot of years left in him, he was essentially in permanent retirement. When the Bums were still touring and making those four albums, every single one of them just MURDERED—like, hit after hit after hit—and they used "Broken Sparrow" in all those Hyundai commercials—probably at this point, it's gotta be like, a hundred?—so we're talking about millions and millions of dollars. And so Chris just had no reason to ever pick up a guitar again unless he really, really wanted to. And he didn't. LOL. He was just like: I'm gonna drink my daiquiris, and get involved at the Seaside Club, and go pick my kids up from school every afternoon, and, every once in a while, we'll go skiing in Colorado, and that's gonna be my life.

But still, I just had it lodged in my mind—I don't know

why, but I was just so obsessed with this idea—that if I could somehow manage to pull Chris Jeffries out of retirement and make some music with him, it was gonna be the dopest shit ever, and so I started talking to him.

And at first, obviously, he was super-dismissive. Like, I didn't dance around it at all—I don't know, I just think something I've learned from Bob is like: Life is too short to bullshit your way through any conversation—and so I just launched right in with: I wanna make a song with you. And Chris was just immediately, like, laughing his ass off. Like, I think his reaction was like: Look at the balls on *this* kid, you know? But I started talking to him about grunge—like, I started talking to him about the scene way back in the day—and he ended up actually being really impressed with the depth of my knowledge. I mean, it's sad, you know, because this meeting would've been the highlight of my dad's life—like, he literally would've *killed* to be at this meeting—but looking back on it now, if my dad ever *did* end up meeting Chris Jeffries, he would've just totally blown it, because he would've brought this energy with him that would've been completely the opposite of what Chris responds to. Like, yeah, my dad was able to keep his cool and sort of keep up his chill vibe in the beginning when it came to our stuff, but my dad actually LOOKED UP to Chris, you know?—like, Chris was his IDOL—and so he would've just turned into this nervous, anxious, horrible little guy, and Chris would've sniffed it out immediately.

But anyway, after a little while talking to him, Chris decided that I was pretty legit. Like, he made up his mind that I was at least knowledgeable and appreciative of the music he had made and the scene he came up in, and so he kind of warmed up to me. And, I mean, he was still sort of joking around, you know, like he was still smiling about it, but eventually, he was just like: Why don't you show me what you've been working on?

And obviously, I had the files on my phone. I brought a pair of headphones with me for exactly this reason, and so I loaded up the demos, and I gave Chris the headphones, and I just watched as he listened to them, like, sipping his daiquiri. He didn't move his head at all—it was just like, very serious, very stoic—and after I played him the first song, he was just like: Is there another one? And so I played him another one. And after that one, he was like: Is there another one? And I played him another one. And he kept doing that until I played him all the songs, and after the last song, he took the headphones out of his ears, and he handed them to me, and he took a long, sort of contemplative sip of his daiquiri, and he was just like: These are great. LOL. This is some of the best shit I've heard in years. And I was just like: Boom. I mean, I've honestly never felt so good showing anything to anybody. It was like the whole sky opened up, and I could see the ocean over the hedges of the Seaside Club, and the sun was glinting just perfectly onto the pool, and for a moment, it was like the Seaside Club was the best place on Earth. I completely understood why Chris loved it so much.

And it turned out that Chris was actually a big fan of the songs I had recorded with Deez for *HERE we Go*. He didn't even know it was me at the time, but apparently when they first came out, he was like, obsessed with them for a couple of weeks—he kept listening to them on repeat and singing them in the car with his kids—and at first he was kind of embarrassed about it, but after a while, he was just like: No, this is some of the best shit in recent memory. This is the real deal. And so it was pretty clear that we had at least been vibing on the same frequency for a while.

And, you know, I left the meeting without a definite commitment from Chris, but I was feeling pretty confident. At a certain point, I guess we had been hanging out for a while and we lost track of the time, and he was like: Shit, I gotta pick my kids up from school. And so we called it a day. But he said he'd be in touch with me, and I gave him my info, and then, like, a week later, I got a call from him, and he was like: Yo, you want to come over today? And I was just, like: Yeah, Chris, I think I can clear my schedule. LOL.

I mean, it's amazing, because he never used it except to like, listen to records and hang out most of the time, but Chris had the most beautiful recording studio in his house. It was just like, a work of art. He had all of these completely amazing guitars hanging up on the wall and like, this beautiful wood paneling all over the place, and all of this old-school, super-high-quality equipment. And he was telling me when I got there that like, only two or three days out of every year, he'd find himself coming down there and recording stuff. Sometimes it'd be full songs, and like, sometimes it'd just be little scraps. And like, he wouldn't really show them to anybody— he'd just record them and put them on a hard drive and forget about them until the next year when he'd come down and record some more—but he'd been doing that basically every year since he stopped putting out records. And I heard that, and I was just like: Chris, we're gonna listen to that shit right now. And Chris was just like: Eh, I don't know. I don't know. I mean, he was being sort of evasive and private about the whole thing, and I was just, like, putting my foot down, like: No, come on, man, you've gotta play me some of this shit. I need to hear it. And so he shuffled over to the laptop he had in there, and he like, hooked it up to the speakers, and he started picking files at random. They didn't even have titles or anything—they just had dates—and he was flicking through them like they were nothing special at all—just like he was watching YouTube videos or something—and some of them were like, thirty seconds long and some of them were like twenty minutes long, and in the middle of one of the songs he was playing for me, I just started crying. Like legit not just tearing up a little bit, but like, actual, literal sobbing. And Chris stopped the track and asked me if I was okay, and I was just like: Yes. Yes. Keep playing it. And so that's the song that eventually became "Upright Citizen." He took down one of the guitars from the wall and started playing the melody, and I just started to riff a little bit and harmonize with it a little bit and sing some words, and after a few hours of us tinkering around, I was like: I think we need to get Trick on this. And Chris just laughed like: You're crazy, man. But I could tell at that point that he was really beginning to trust my sensibility, and so he let me call Trick over, and when Trick came in and heard what we had been doing, he was like: Oh my fucking God. I mean, Trick just went nuts. First of all, like, he had never even seen Chris's studio—in all their years of knowing each other, he had never been invited in—but then, like, when he heard what we were working on, it was just like, this volcano of creativity just got released from him, and he started going crazy in the booth. Like, he was basically producing the tracks live and bringing in samples and modulating the pitch and creating beats, like literally crafting beats right there in front of us. And we basically just stayed in there for sixteen hours straight building the song and then working on some other ones—I mean, it was like, we'd take bits of the shit I had written, and we'd take bits of the shit Chris had written, and then Trick would just sort of meld them all together and bring some of his own vibe—and literally the only reason we even thought to take a break is that at a certain point, Chris was just like: Guys, if I don't go to the bathroom right now, I'm gonna shit all over the floor. And so we all went upstairs, and we all went to the bathroom, and we ordered some Thai food, and then, like, we went right back into it—like, legitimately, I think we were in there together for maybe thirty-six hours—and by the end of it, we had a fucking album. Like, yeah, there were still some little touches to be put here and there, and like, yeah, we still had to master the thing, but at the end of that thirty-six-hour session, we had basically finished the album I ended up putting out as *Roses and Mud*. And so the album became this sort of crazy hybrid thing, where like, half of the tracks were these uber-quiet, uber-delicate piano songs I had recorded in France, and half of them were these insane collaborations I did with Chris and Trick in Chris's studio. And I remember just listening to the completed album for the first time and thinking: What the fuck are people gonna think about this? Like, I actually had no idea how any of it was gonna go over. But then, like, I mean, I think the only way to accurately describe what it was like when we dropped it was like it was a *seismic* shift, you know? It felt like we had actually changed the game. Like we had actually reached a new benchmark and created a new sound that like, people were going to have to reckon with forever. And that was honestly some new territory for me. I mean, I had *killed it* before, you know—like, I had felt before like I had pushed things forward a little bit or pushed some boundaries here and there—but this was a whole new thing. This was like, *historical*. And I don't mean to sound like I'm bragging or something, because really, it almost feels like it wasn't even *me* that did it. I mean, I don't subscribe to that bullshit at all—that, like, "the spirit spoke through me" bullshit—but it's funny, because you *do* end up believing in something like magic. Like, so many artists I know, so many creative people are the most superstitious people on the planet, because how else do you explain what happened in that room between me and Chris and Trick? The only thing I can say is that something *magical* happened. Some force took over. And I don't necessarily need to examine it that much further, but I would be lying if I said that I totally understood it. To this day, I still think about that time as this insane dream I had, or like, this insane alien abduction that I'm not even sure really took place. But the memory is so vivid, and the evidence is so clear, and the effect it had is so undeniable that like, all I can do is just look at the results and go: Wow. That happened. Wow.

. . .

Right now in the video game, we're trying to figure out how to deal with my dad's suicide.

We've gotten to the point where you've made all the choices that lead you up to that moment in France, where like, I'm recording all of the piano songs for *Roses and Mud* and I get that message on my phone from my dad with that crazy cover of the song with Deez, and then it's like: What do you do from there, you know? What are your options?

We're trying to figure out the decision tree for that moment. Which things at that point would've led to my dad not killing himself? What would've happened then?

I don't believe in fate or whatever—part of the point of the whole game, you know, is to remind people that we're always in charge of our lives, there's no big puppet master who's making all the decisions for us—but there is this part of me that sort of feels like my dad HAD to die when he did, you know what I mean? Like, now that I'm sitting there with Roger and Ines, like, actually thinking through the possibilities, it just feels like the only real way it could've gone down is the way that it actually went down in real life. I guess it's just one of those things that once it happens, it sort of gets locked into your reality, you know?—locked into the fabric of time—and so it seems like the world was always leading up to it.

But we're having a tough time figuring out all those different options, and it's also a problem because, you know, like I said, every time we try to add more options and expand the world, we have to sacrifice something else because the engine can't take it. Like, the graphics look kind of janky already, and it's like, I don't really care THAT much about it—you know, like, I don't need it to be the *prettiest* game on the market—but it still feels like a bummer to roll out something that looks like shit. That would just be kind of disappointing to me, you know, as an artist.

One option I came up with the other day is like: Instead of ignoring all those Content Bucket videos, you start watching them obsessively after you receive my dad's message, and like, you start looking for clues about where he is. And if you watch them all really closely, you can see that there's this one video he made where there's a glitch on the green screen—like, this actually happened. He didn't frame it perfectly this one time, and so a corner of the basement wall was just peeking out—and you can see on the wall that there's this little bicycle rack that my dad made when I was eight that I guess the people who lived there after us never took down from the wall.

And so once you spot that, the option comes up to travel to St. James. And you get on the next flight out from where you're staying in France, and you rush to your old house, and you burst into the basement while my dad is in the middle of recording one of those videos, or like, maybe you burst into my old room as my dad is starting to load the shotgun, and you scream out: DAD! Or something. And you rush up to him and you give him a hug and you say: Stop! Stop. I'm here now. It's all gonna be okay.

Or maybe you've brought your guitar with you, you know—in the video game, there's an option to start taking the lessons earlier—and so you burst into the room and my dad is looking at you, like, completely shocked and surprised that you found him, and you just take out the guitar and you start playing the chords for the song that he sent you. And he gets out his guitar and he plays along with you. And the two of you, like, right there in the old house in St. James, start making music together again, you know? You decide to work together again on the next album—just a father, a son, and their guitars.

I don't know.

I have to think a little more about it.

I don't want it to feel lame or whatever.

#17—Bottom of my left foot. This is the logo from *The Midnight Gang*. I was on the show a few years ago with Deez and Skelet0r—I think we must have been promoting *b00mbuck$*, Deez's album—and we played this game of charades where, like, if the hosts of the show lost, they'd have to get the name of the album tattooed somewhere on their bodies, and if we lost, we'd have to get the show's logo tattooed somewhere on our bodies. And, obviously, we lost. Skelet0r sucks at charades. LOL.

#96—Right bicep. This is a little EKG machine showing a regular heartbeat. When Amelia was born, she had this heart condition—I forget what it was exactly, but it was super-serious—and they had to have her on a machine for a few weeks before Patrick and Gloria could even take her home, and so Patrick was freaking out and losing his mind during that whole time. She's fine now, but on the day they finally released her from the hospital with a working heart, I decided to go get this tat just to show Patrick and Gloria that I was thinking about them.

#87—Right shoulder. This is a camera and a boom mic, and I got it the week they started filming *The Winstocks*.

I actually don't want to talk about it too much here, because I kind of think that's gross—like, I don't really want this to seem like a *cross-promotional* sort of thing, and if you're reading this, you've probably already decided that you're gonna watch the show when it drops—but I guess I just feel like I should mention it, since this is the "story of my life," and it'd be weird if I left it out.

A few months ago, this producer approached Bob with the idea of doing a reality show about his life in L.A. Basically, the pitch was like: You're this incredibly controversial figure, everybody thinks they know who you are, everyone thinks they know what you stand for, but what if we could show people the other side of Bob Winstock? What if we could show people the Bob Winstock who's a husband and a father and a stepfather, and what if you could tell people who you are in your own words?

And, at first, I think Bob sort of thought the idea was ridiculous—we all did—but after he talked it over with my mom and thought about it for a while, I think he started to get really excited about all of the different possibilities it presented just in terms of reaching out to people, you know? Making his ideas connect.

I remember when Bob and my mom first talked to me about it and I was just like: No. LOL. I really didn't want them to do it. They both seemed so excited about it, and I was just like: Why would you guys want to do this? Why would this be something you're interested in? And my mom started saying how it would be really good for raising the profile of her jewelry brand and how it'd be really good for Bob's books, and I was like: Yeah, but you guys are doing fine. We're all doing fine. None of us needs the money. And Bob was like: It's not about the money. It's about connection. Nobody reads my books. Nobody actually knows what I've written there. Even most of the people who *buy* the books don't read them. And that's fine. I've been at peace with that for a while. But what if I could talk to people in a medium they understand? What if I could meet them in a medium they're comfortable with? I'm trying to write philosophy about *today*—I'm trying to talk to people *today*—and yet the only way most people experience me or my ideas is through what they hear about me on talk shows or what they read about me on the internet. Why wouldn't I try to create the narrative myself? And I was like: But how are you gonna do philosophy on a reality show? And Bob was like: The same way I do it in life. The same way I do it with you. I'm just gonna exist. So is your mom. So is Lenny. We're all just gonna show people what it's like to be free.

And I looked at the two of them, and I saw how excited they both were, and I kind of felt like if it wasn't their place to tell me not to make a video game or not to make a grunge album, then it definitely wasn't my place to tell them not to make their reality show, and so I smiled and hugged them both, and I was like: When do we start?

And, you know, in the end, it hasn't really affected *my*

life that much. I mean, I'm ON the show, obviously, but I made it clear to everyone that I wasn't gonna have my own camera crew and that I was only gonna be a part of it when I could—like, I was only gonna show up on the show when I was over at their place—and they were all pretty cool with that. Every once in a while, the producers will bug my manager about it or text me and be like: *Hey, you haven't gone over to your mom's house in a while . . .* But I've been able to make it work for my schedule.

And, I mean, it's actually been kind of exciting, you know, because Bob has been pouring his whole soul into this thing. Like, he's honestly not even writing that much anymore. I think he's really started to see it as the next step for him, the next logical frontier for the kind of work he's been trying to do. In all the time I've known him, I've never seen him so dedicated to anything.

And my mom in her own way seems really excited about it too. I mean, it's actually kind of cute, because at first it was clear that she was really uncomfortable in front of the cameras—I mean, she's not like me or Bob, you know? She's never been a public person—and so the team actually had to work with her a lot just to get her to chill out and be herself, but I think she's been settling into it really well over the filming of the first season. Every time I go over there and hang out with them, I can tell that my mom is relaxing a lot more and having a lot more fun, and it seems like she's gotten really chill with the camera people and the producers.

And Bob, I mean, in a way it's like the show is the perfect platform for him to express himself, you know? Something I'm hoping the show is gonna do is just let people see what it's like to hang out with Bob, just shoot the shit. Honestly, more than anything he's ever written, that's always been what's important to me. I'm hoping the show will sort of open people up to him and make it easier for them to let him into their lives and look past all the shit they think they know about him. I mean, obviously, when the show was first announced, there were a lot of people being like: Why would you support this guy? Why would you give this guy a platform? But I'm hoping once people start actually watching the show, they'll see the same Bob I see: the goofball Bob, the generous Bob, the Bob who's never been anything other than an amazing husband to my mom and an amazing dad to my brother.

There's also obviously still a lot of people who have complicated feelings about what this all means for Lenny—like, whether it's ethical to be raised in front of the cameras from basically age one—but I've honestly come to think of it like: Lenny was never gonna have a "normal" life, you know? That was never in the cards for him. Not with these parents. Not with this brother. And what the fuck *is* a normal life anyway? Maybe the *most* normal life you could have, the most normal life possible, is one where you've got cameras shoved in your face right from the start. Maybe it'll actually be *good* for Lenny to have all these memes being made about him before he's even conscious, before he even understands what it means to be alive. The only difference between Lenny and anyone else is that he won't ever be able to pretend it's not happening, you know? He won't ever be able to pretend that it doesn't come naturally. By the time he grows up, it'll just be part of the environment, part of the air. And maybe it'll eventually just be *nothing*. What kind of freedom would that be? What kind of power is that? Maybe Lenny is the prototype for a whole new kind of human. Maybe when people say they're worried about him, all they really mean is that they're afraid of evolving as a species.

Oddvar emailed me today.

They had a big flood at the seed vault, and they had to move some of the seeds around and reseal the entryway. He wanted to let me know that all of the seeds are safe—including the ones they named after me—but they might have to rework the structure of the building and maybe even think about moving it somewhere else to prevent this from happening again. The seed vault was supposed to last forever—you know, like, even in the case of some crazy emergency where there was like, a worldwide power outage or a nuclear war or something, the permafrost in the mountain was supposed to naturally keep the building frozen at a certain temperature until the end of time—but now the world is heating up so fast that the permafrost is actually *melting*, and so Oddvar and his team are just like: WTF? Two days ago, they woke up, and there was just this *river* of ice water gushing into the entryway. All of these alarms started going off, and this one dude almost drowned.

NONE of these guys thought this was possible, you know? Like, these are the guys who are supposed to know more about this shit than anybody else, and even *they* were just like: Whoa. Shit. I've honestly never heard Oddvar so bummed. I mean, it was just an email and like, usually his emails are kind of formal and serious-sounding, but this one was really sort of hopeless, and like, actually sort of sad. I mean, I don't want to make it sound like Oddvar's *depressed* or something, because like, he's one of the most optimistic people I know—I mean, when you think about it, his whole project is one big bet on the future—but reading his email today—like, seeing the way he was describing everything—he just seemed like the kind of sad that you can only really get if you're also sort of shocked, you know what I mean? I could just feel him coming to accept the possibility that maybe we really *are* all doomed and that maybe there really *isn't* anything we can do about it.

It's funny because, like, Bob's whole take on global warming is that we should just let it happen. LOL. I mean, he totally believes in it—like, he's one hundred percent on board with the idea that it's our fault and that we're the ones causing it—but he just sort of thinks that there's obviously nothing we can do to stop it at this point, and so we might as well let 'er rip and see where it takes us. Like, we're obviously not even really making a dent, and so we should be preparing for the worst instead of holding on to this bullshit hope. And Bob is sort of cautiously optimistic that like, when the shit really does start hitting the fan, it's gonna be so crazy and like, so horrible that we'll actually take a step back for a second and rethink the whole thing—like, we'll actually start back from square one and go: Okay, where did we go wrong last time? How can we do it differently this time?—but he's also the first to admit that like, there's only a small chance that'll happen. More likely, it'll just be a total shitshow.

When I talked to Oddvar about all this at the seed vault, his opinion wasn't actually that different from Bob's. I mean, he disagreed that there was nothing we could do about it, or that like, we shouldn't at least *try*, but he was saying that what Bob definitely gets right is that like, most of the people who *say* that they're concerned about global warming are just totally fucking full of shit or like, at the very least, just completely fucking stupid.

While Oddvar was in the middle of giving us the tour last week, I noticed that there was this giant cupboard filled with bottled water near the kitchen, and I was like, kind of joking, like: Whoa, Oddvar, I thought you guys were supposed to be all eco-friendly and shit. And Oddvar just looked at me, and he smiled for a second, and then he made that jerk-off motion in the air. You know what I'm talking about? That, like, motion, where you do a few quick jerks and then you let the jizz fly all over the room?

But it's actually kind of nuts, because like, one of the rooms that got flooded—one of the rooms that was almost filled to the top with ice water when the permafrost melted—was the guest room where me and the boys had been staying. I'm calling it a "guest room," but it was really just like, a closet with a few bunk beds. And, legitimately, if we had gone and visited him this week instead of last week, we would've been sleeping in there when the ceiling caved in and all of this ice water just started gushing in through the cracks. We might've actually drowned or something. I mean, it's no fucking joke.

In his email, Oddvar was SO apologetic about it. He was just like—I don't know, I think it's been really eating him up inside that he put me in that kind of a situation.

Like, the seed vault getting destroyed is one thing, but losing me or being responsible for my injury or my death is just not really something I think Oddvar can handle. He was saying crazy shit like: I understand if you never want to speak with me again. And: I hate myself for what I've done to you. And: Forget about me. You owe me nothing but scorn. And I just wrote him back being like: Whoa, Oddvar, chill out, you know? It was an honest mistake. You can't apologize for *nature*. Like, yeah, you're supposed to know more about this shit than the rest of us, but like, we're all just *ants* in the grand scheme of things. We can't control the *ice*. I mean, honestly, what I told him was like: If that's how I go—if I literally get KILLED by global warming—I think I can live with that. LOL. Of all the ways I've imagined dying, that one's actually pretty next-level.

But I don't know. I guess I find myself being an optimist in the long run. It just seems so obvious to me that we're gonna figure it out somehow. Like, you look at the history of humanity, and you look at what we've been able to accomplish, and it's like, yeah, there was some really stupid, really selfish and destructive shit, but every couple years, we just get a legit *genius*, you know? We've legitimately produced so many geniuses when you think about it—even just in the past century. And I mean, it wasn't that long ago when we didn't even have *electricity*, you know? It wasn't that long ago when everybody thought Earth was the center of the universe. And now, like, some aboriginal tribe in some tiny corner of the globe can watch my videos on their phones and send messages to each other by bouncing signals off of satellites in space, and so it just seems crazy to me that someone's not gonna figure out how we can stop warming the planet. I'm pretty convinced that some genius is going to stumble onto the scene one of these days, and just be like: Oh, dope, I solved it. Like, they won't even be trying to, you know what I mean? They'll just be working around in the lab one day, like, trying to do something else entirely, and then they'll get some crazy result on their machine and they'll be like: Whoa. Shit.

Because like, I've experienced some version of that in the studio, you know? Like, what I did with Chris and Trick—I'm not saying our music solved global warming— but if music COULD solve global warming, like, if music had that kind of power, we would've done it that day together. I know that sounds fucking crazy, but whatever: I'm over it. I'm already over whatever reaction you're gonna have to the way that sounds.

All I'm saying is: There's got to be some scientist who's on the verge of some major breakthrough. There has to be some person who's just like, right on the brink of making a life-changing discovery that's gonna save us all. And, who knows? Maybe they haven't even been born yet. Maybe it's some kid who hasn't even been conceived. Or maybe it'll be Oddvar. Maybe he'll just be running tests one day in the seed vault and like, going out and digging holes in the ice or whatever he does and taking measurements, and then he'll just be like: Of course! You know? It's always something so obvious. In the movies, whenever they're showing a scientist coming to some next-level realization, it's always something that's been right under their nose this whole time. And then they figure it out by accident and they're just like: How could I have been so stupid? How could I have ignored this?

#32—Left shoulder. A lot of people think this one's an angel, but it's actually a character from Bob's book *The Question of Society*. It was the first novel that he ever wrote—like, way back when he was in his twenties—and it was one of the first things of his I ever read. There's this character, Barbie-One-6-3, who goes flying around the city—she's a robot with mechanical wings—and she eats people's brains whenever they've outlived their purpose, like, according to the society. It was a pretty dark book, but I just thought that character was super-scary, you know, and like, if I had her on my shoulder, no one could fuck with me. Plus, like, hardly anyone's ever read that book, and so most people just see the tat and think it's this really cute angel or something, which I think is hilarious.

#54—Right arm. This is Jason Gideon, the like, main detective from that TV show *Criminal Minds*. I forget the name of the actor who plays him—he was only on the show for like, two or three seasons—but I just always felt a deep connection to this guy. When we were touring with the first album, I was just watching a TON of that show on the bus, and I would always see that character and think like: *This* is how a person's supposed to be. LOL. *This* is a *man*. And there's this amazing thing that they do at the end of every episode where like, they have the crew coming back from catching a serial killer or solving a murder or whatever, and they're just riding the private jet back to the FBI headquarters, and for the first time all episode, you see them super-relaxed, like, actually getting to talk to each other and hang out and be themselves, because they know, like, as long as they're up in the air, as long as they're above civilization, all that danger, all that stress in the world can't touch them. And that just really reminded me of what it's like in the jet with me and Curt and Patrick and Mo, you know? Up in the air and out in the middle of the ocean—those are the two places where we can really chill and be ourselves. Between the two, though, the air is better, because I've seen paparazzi people just pop out of the fucking surface of the water, like, in a submarine or some shit, trying to take pictures of me on the yacht. Seriously! I've seen them do it! But unless they're fucking military trained, I doubt they'll be able to fly alongside us and board our plane.

#49—Left wrist. I've gotten into a lot of trouble for this one. I guess because it's in Arabic? Like, I guess there are a lot of people in the world who are like: Why would you have that language on your body? Why would you support that language? And it's like: You realize it's a *language*, right? You realize it's just WORDS? I remember right after I got it and posted a picture of it, everyone was freaking out being like: WHAT DOES IT MEAN? WHAT DOES IT SAY? WHAT KIND OF HIDDEN MESSAGE IS THIS? And people were coming up with all these crazy theories. And then finally this dude from Syria just wrote in the comments, like: All it says is "Love & Justice," people. Chill.

. . .

I got it as a tribute to Mandy. Not in a lovey-dovey way, but like, just as a tribute to what she was going through and what she was doing. I wanted to find a way that I could support her, you know? Show her that I had her back.

After we got back from France, like, while I was doing all the *Roses and Mud* shit and gearing up to tour with Chris and Trick, Mandy was definitely in a better place about what had happened in Berlin than she was like, in the days immediately following the attacks, but she still wasn't "over it," and she still wasn't resolved in her mind about what had happened or why it had happened, and so I think she started to go really deep into all of the various explanations she could find.

Mandy is actually this incredibly smart, incredibly deep person. Like, people might not assume that because of the early music that she was putting out, or like, they might watch those interviews from the *L.A. Baby* days or like, look at the *Heartache/Heartbreak* music videos and think they know who she is, but the truth is, she's actually always been this really complex thinker, and she just sort of compartmentalized all that shit so that it wouldn't get in the way of her career. Like, it was always so clear to me that like, Mandy got to L.A. when she was thirteen or whatever, and she saw what the game was and she saw how it worked, and she was just sort of like: Okay. Got it. And then that same level of *perfection* that she brought to her voice—like, that same thing that makes her voice so spotless—she brought to the whole thing, you know? The interviews, the outfits, the videos, the charity work: All of it was just sort of untouchable. There were never any blemishes. Which was kind of the thing that started to annoy me about it, or like, the thing that I started to really dislike about the shit she was making, because it just always felt sort of *lifeless*, or like I couldn't see *Mandy* in it. But at the same time, Mandy and her team were actually really smart because she was just so *reliable*, you know? Mandy was maybe never the person who was getting the MOST attention or like, making the MOST headlines or raking in the MOST money, but she was ALWAYS killing it. She was consistently putting out shit that was doing well, and like, when someone else would fuck up big time or like, when someone else would take a wrong turn or say the wrong thing or make a fool of themselves and drop out of the game, Mandy was always there to fill in the gaps. And even when she did all the sexy stuff, you know, like, even when she took that leap into adulthood and adult music and started showing more skin and singing about wanting to get fucked or wanting to get "dirty," like, even then, she was still doing it in a way where you could listen to it with your mom and your grandma in the car and none of you would be embarrassed when the song was over. It was definitely sexy and it was definitely hot—like, if you watch the video for "Take Me" or "Like I Want You" or really anything from *Mobilize*, there's no denying that it's all sexy as hell—but at the end of the day, she could still show up to the Kidz Spot Awards and none of the parents were gonna be upset that she was presenting.

And so as a result of all that, you know, like, up until that thing happened in Berlin, I don't really think Mandy was ever concerned with like, politics or history or any of that shit, because as far as she was concerned, it was only ever gonna get in the way. Like, in her mind, the costs of getting mixed up in that shit were always gonna outweigh the benefits. But then that thing happened in Berlin, and it was like, I mean, in a lot of ways it was sort of an *awakening* for her, because she had to reconcile all of this horrible anger and violence in the world with all of the shit that she thought her music and her shows were supposed to be about, which was love and peace and happiness and acceptance.

It wasn't enough of an explanation for her that what had happened was just like, some crazy evil. That's kind of what everybody was trying to tell her—I mean, even *I* was trying to tell her that for a while, that, like, you can't get caught up in this shit, because there's just a lot of evil in the world and it's really unfortunate that it knocked on your doorstep, but it's got nothing to do with you—but Mandy was like: No. There's gotta be a reason for this. There's gotta be an explanation for why this happened beyond like, "some people are just crazy." And so she started doing all this research.

I mean, Mandy really would've made an amazing high school teacher—maybe even a college professor or something—because she's such an *academic* when it comes down to it. Like, when she gets into something, she gets in *deep*. She's such a good student. Back when we were together, she was reading constantly—she was obsessed with all that vampire shit, like *the Dying Dawn* series or *Sisters of the Blood*, but she wouldn't just read the books, you know? She would look up all these historical accounts of vampire sightings and like, get into all this scholarship about what vampires *symbolize* in *literature*—but now, like, after all the stuff with her concert happened, she just wanted to find out where the guys who did it were from and like, what their motivations were, and how they possibly could've gotten to a place in their minds where it made sense for them to do this, and so she read everything she could get her hands on. She wasn't gonna stop until it all made sense to her.

And at first, you know, she was doing it all in secret—like, she wasn't really making it public that she was trying to educate herself about all this shit—but then as she got deeper and deeper into it, and like, as she started to really put together a picture for herself of like, what exactly had gone wrong in the world so that something like this was even possible, she started to want to share it with people, because it felt like, I don't know, I guess she sort of felt a responsibility, you know, as someone whose concert created the environment for something like this to happen.

And I mean, I think people were expecting a particular sort of response after Mandy returned to the public eye. Like, everybody was sort of cool with Mandy disappearing for a bit and gathering her thoughts, but I think they all assumed that when she finally *did* resurface, she would say something like: I'm so sorry for all the lives that have been lost, and I hope we can react to this horrible tragedy with love instead of hate. But instead, you know, when Mandy finally did come out and say something, she was talking about Western imperial aggression, and fucking drone strikes, and, like, the history of regime change in the Middle East, and people were just like: WHOA. I mean, they were just like: *What the fuck?* It really took them by surprise.

I even saw conspiracy theories online saying that Mandy was *in on the attacks*, you know, and that like, she had helped the terrorists *plan them*, and it was like: People were NOT fucking happy. People were really losing their minds.

And it's not like Mandy was trying to shock anybody or anything. I mean, it's not like Mandy was saying what she was saying to be controversial or to make people upset or to piss people off. I really hated that, actually, when people were saying shit like Mandy was doing this as a *marketing strategy* or, like, she was trying to "rebrand" herself as some radical or something, because the truth was actually so much simpler. It was just like, she did all the research, and she came to her conclusions, and she was like: This is obviously the truth, and so I should obviously be saying it. And it started to feel like NOT addressing all this shit, like, NOT fully examining all the causes of what happened—like, just giving the sort of measured and careful and meaningless statement that everybody was expecting her to give—would've actually been the *political* thing to do, because as far as Mandy was concerned, that would've been the thing that would've required her to have an angle. The way she saw it, she was just stating the facts.

And I think the most upset people got, you know, like, the thing that really pissed a lot of people off was that like, before Mandy even went and visited some of the families of the victims—like, before she even went and saw all the people who were still in the hospital—she went and visited the mother of the guys who had done it.

They were two brothers, and they grew up in Germany, but, you know, they had all this family in Yemen. And they weren't even particularly religious or whatever—like, the mom said that they weren't even that conservative—but a year or two before the attacks happened, a bunch of their cousins got killed in a drone strike for like, apparently no reason at all—like, apparently, they were just walking down the street one day, and then: *BOOM*. They were gone—and the mom told Mandy that this thing really did a number on her sons. Like, apparently, it was all they could talk about for a while. And the mom didn't know it—or like, that's what she says. There's a lot of people in the newspapers and online who think she's full of shit—but the mom *said* at least that she had no idea that like, in the time between their cousins dying and the sons carrying out the attack, they were just getting completely indoctrinated online. And anyway, they were able to get their hands on some guns and get tickets to the concert and somehow get through the security and then, like, you know, that was that.

And I mean, obviously, Mandy wasn't coming out and saying that she SUPPORTED what these guys had done. Like, obviously, Mandy was totally horrified by all this stuff, and she thought that what these guys did was the worst possible way to respond to all that horrible shit that had happened to them and their country and their family, but still like, I think Mandy was sort of determined to use this thing as a way to grow as a person, you know, and to understand the world a little better. One of the first things she did was to come out and plead with people to see this thing in its larger context. She posted this thing online that said like, this didn't happen in a vacuum, and if we want to condemn *this* act of violence, we need to all examine *all* of our individual and collective roles in perpetuating violence around the world. And at the end of the post, she pleaded with the German government to go easy on the brother they were able to capture and try to actually rehabilitate him and understand him, you know, instead of just punishing him.

And I mean, you know, Mandy wasn't about to pretend like she was an expert on all this shit, but I think it's kind of crazy that even her *attempt* to understand, you know, like, even her *suggestion* that maybe there was something a little deeper going on here than just "these dudes were crazy" was met with such backlash and resistance. Even Mandy's own family, like, practically disowned her. Not her mom, obviously. Kelly would never do something like that. But Mandy's grandpa, like, went on air and did an interview where he was like: This is not the granddaughter I loved and cared for. This is not my kin. And it was just like: Whoa, man, WTF?

But, you know, Mandy was just sort of like: Who gives a fuck? I mean, really, all of this shit sort of unleashed this amazing well of strength in her that I had never seen before, because she was just like: Who *cares* what people are saying about me? We live in a *fake world*. We're part of a *fake world*. I'm trying to talk about something *real*.

The same Mandy who, just a few years ago, was afraid of being associated with Bob because of all the shit he had said about gay people was now, like, playing shows in refugee camps, and going to antiwar protests, and wearing a bandanna with the Palestinian flag at her concerts, and posting all these interviews she'd conducted online with like, all of these sort of radical intellectuals from around the world, and it's like, yeah, she's definitely lost a few fans, but it's been kind of amazing to watch how all these new people have come out of the woodwork, like, all these new fans who never used to give a shit about Mandy who are now all of a sudden so excited to hear about what she's doing. She's been getting interviewed in all these magazines—like, the same ones that call Bob "the most dangerous man in America"—and it's just like: Wow, you know? Who would've predicted *this*?

And, you know, nobody really knew that Mandy had tats—like, I don't think people even really knew about the seagull that she had above her heart because she kept that shit really private: Her image was still so clean and so pure, and like, her people weren't sure that tats were a good fit for that—but when she started getting all these tattoos in Arabic and people were freaking out about it, I was just watching it all unfold, and one day, I was like: Fuck it. What's the big fucking deal?

And so I went out and called up Optimus, and I was like: Yo, do you know anyone who speaks Arabic? And Optimus was like: Nah, not really, but I could look something up. And I was like: Hold on a second. Let me call Mandy.

And so I called her, and I was like: Hey, come to Optimus's place and let's get matching tattoos.

And Mandy came by, and we sat in the chairs, and she didn't even tell me what our tattoos meant until after the ink was settling in. I didn't even ask. She just gave the template to Optimus, and he did the tats on both of us, and then when he was done, Mandy looked at me, and she said: Love & Justice.

And I was like: Dope.

And then a few days later, my skin was still healing as I got on the plane with Chris and Trick and we took off for the start of the *Roses and Mud* tour.

And everybody knows how *that* went.

LOL.

I guess we might as well get into it.

At first, you know, it seemed like we were off to a good start. The press and the excitement and all of the love and exposure we were getting for the album was pretty cool, and Chris was really enjoying it, you know, like, he was sort of happy to have a chance to feel what that was like again: to be on top of the world again, not as some twenty-one-year-old from Portland, but as a fully grown man with a family and a home and some perspective on everything. And, at first, like, he was just really grateful for the opportunity to be playing new music again and to be caught up in the energy and the excitement of having made something that people were responding to.

I remember at one of the early shows, Chris was just so surprised by how *nice* everything was, you know? He was so surprised by, like, how well everybody took care of themselves. Like, I remember before one of our big early shows—I think we were playing some festival in the UK—we were backstage, and Chris was just looking around at everybody, and he was like: NO ONE is high. Like, it hadn't even occurred to me that that was weird, but Chris was looking around at all of these people with like, their coconut waters and their yoga mats and like, their vegan quinoa bowls, and he was just like: How the fuck can this be a music festival? And I looked around a bit, and I saw the Pizza Boyz, and I was like: What about those guys? Those guys are blazed as hell. And Chris was like: Yeah, those people are *stoned*, but nobody's HIGH. Nobody's off the fucking ground. Twenty years ago, this place would've looked like a war zone.

And he was right. I mean, I guess by the time I got into the game, the scene had already changed completely from Chris's time, but these days, no one is getting *trashed* before a show. Like, that's just not really something that you can do. If Mandy came out onstage totally trashed or like, if I came out onstage totally trashed, people would just be like: WTF? You know? They'd just be like: What *happened* to you? But for Chris, I mean, when Chris was coming up, that was just par for the course. People were smoking—like everyone, even the singers were smoking three packs a day—and like, people were snorting coke off of toilets and shooting heroin in between sets, and like, it just would've been insane to imagine that twenty years later, there would be a yoga tent and a juice fridge and a meditation room. Like legitimately, at the festival we were playing, there was a tent just for the artists where, like, the festival had hired a yogi to come and lead classes every day, and Chris just thought that was the funniest shit ever. And like, even some of the harder dudes I know—like, even Scaggs or MURDER or Flip Dragon—like even those dudes are taking vitamins and drinking tea and like, resting their vocal cords before a gig. The scene's just changed a lot—it's become a lot healthier. And that's not to say that people don't still lose it a little bit. Like, there are people like KETO or like, Abbi DiFranco who just totally go off the deep end, but when they do, it's not like some proof of how hard-core they are. Instead, it's like, this really sad and pathetic thing that they need to go get HELP for. People are WORRIED for them, you know? And I think Chris was a little shocked by that. I think he was expecting—maybe even hoping for—a little bit of the old danger that used to follow him everywhere he went.

And so, you know, for the first time in my whole career, I found myself doing shots before gigs. It started out pretty harmless. It was sort of like this big joke: like, Chris would make fun of me and Trick and the backup singers and the road crew for being such little pussies, and he'd say shit like: Come on, it's just one shot. I thought you were musicians. And so we'd all do it and laugh about it and it would be fine, but as the tour went on, like, one shot turned into two shots and two shots into three shots, and pretty soon the rest of us were like: Chris, we can't keep up with you. You do whatever you want to do, but the rest of us just can't perform like this. And I think that made Chris feel a little isolated.

It's not like it all turned into a problem immediately. Chris is a pretty champion drinker—I mean, those aren't *virgin* daiquiris at the Seaside Club—so at first, like, yeah, it was a little worrying how much he was putting away before the shows, but he was still able to make it onstage and do his thing and give a great performance and hit all the notes and be in good enough shape at the end of the night to make it back to his hotel room and call his wife and pass out. But somewhere around when we made it back to the U.S.—we started the tour in New York, and then went to Europe and Asia and then we headed back to do, like, a coast-to-coast tour before we left again to play a few more dates abroad—sometime around when we made it back on home soil, the whole flavor of the thing started to change, and Chris just really started to go off the deep end.

Honestly, I think it had a lot to do with the fans. For the first couple shows—for the New York show and the Europe shows and the Asia shows—it was mostly still *my* fans who were showing up—like, it was mostly still people who were there to see ME—and like, yeah, a lot of them had *heard* of Chris, but he wasn't like, this *God* to them in the same way that he was to my dad or my dad's generation. And then as the tour went on, I guess word started to get around that Chris was back—that like, Chris was back to his old ways—and so people started showing up with this really different energy. People started to show up expecting a replay of their experiences from twenty years ago, and Chris just started to feed off of that in the worst possible way.

The first sign that things were really taking a turn for the worse was when we played our show in Portland, and for the first time all tour, the makeup of the crowd was almost half mine and half Chris's. We were expecting that there'd be a big turnout for Chris—obviously, he's a major deal there—but we weren't expecting that they'd come out in *droves*, you know? And I've been pushing boundaries and doing some crazier shit for a while—like, it's been a long time since the *Be My Baby* days—but you've gotta remember, like, there's still this big core of my fan base that's made up of teenagers and their parents. I mean, there's a lot of people showing up to my concerts who are seeing a concert for the first time—it's like twelve-year-olds, ten-year-olds even—and I love that about my shows. I've always loved that the shows belong to everybody. But Chris's fans showed up with this energy of *Us versus Them*, you know? Like, they really seemed to feel like Chris was THEIRS, and like the whole concert was THEIRS, and they weren't going to be happy unless they were able to take over the whole space.

And I mean, I've played shows for sort of rowdy crowds before. Like, at Summer Jamz or whatever, things can get pretty crazy, but these people were throwing things up onto the stage, you know? That had happened to me *once* before, like, when I was playing this show with Scaggs in Detroit, but the worst anybody did was throw up a joint or like, throw up some panties, which, like, Scaggs's security guys would pick up and take backstage in case he wanted to check them out later. But at this Portland show people were throwing little baggies of *cocaine*, you know? People were throwing up *heroin*. And like, fifty-year-old women were flashing their tits and vomiting in the aisles, and I was just like: Whoa. This is not a vibe that I *ever* wanted to be a part of.

But, you know, Chris was loving it. I mean, he was already pretty hammered, but like, once he was out there and he saw how crazy the crowd was getting, he just got this look in his eyes, like—I mean, it was like this thing had been *awakened* in him, you know, this like, ancient, evil spirit—and I just didn't even recognize him anymore. He just summoned his old self—like, he fully brought back the mid-'90s Chris Jeffries—and he let that guy take the steering wheel entirely.

And at the top, he was still doing a pretty good job— like, he was still playing all the notes and remembering all the words to the songs—but as the night went on, he just started to do whatever drugs people would throw up there. Like, someone would throw a little baggie of coke, and Chris would do that, and then like, someone would throw up some pills and Chris would do that. And, like, me and Trick and the rest of the band were just standing there watching all this like: What the fuck are we even supposed to *do*, you know? I mean, we couldn't stop the show or pull the plug or whatever, because there would've been a riot in the auditorium, so we just watched this crazy shit unfolding. And at a certain point, like, people started throwing up drugs that Chris didn't even recognize. Chris would look at the baggie and stop the song and speak into the mic, like: What's this one called? And the person who threw it up would yell "Animal Brains" or whatever, and Chris would do it. And Chris picked up this one baggie, and when he looked at it, he got this smile on his face like: I know what THIS one is. But he spoke into the mic anyway, and he said: What's this one? And some crazy person out in the crowd was like: HEROIN! And Chris just, like, smiled this crazy smile and then put it away in his pocket.

And, that's the only time in my life when I've ever had to issue a formal apology where, like, I actually *meant it*,

JUSTIN KURITZKES

you know? I've had to apologize for some pretty stupid shit over the years, but after that show in Portland, I WANTED to issue an apology. It was like, *I* was the one who called my publicist and was like: What the fuck should we *do* here, you know? You can imagine how horrified some of these parents were who brought their kids to this show. I had no idea a human being could even *take* so many drugs.

And so the next day, we had like, a big conference, like, a big sit-down with Shari and Bobby and the rest of the managers and the publicists, and we were all just like: Chris, this shit can't happen again. This was completely insane. And Chris was just, like, laughing, like: Of course, of course, I was just having a little fun. Just keeping Portland on their toes. Like, he was acting totally fucking crazy. I bet he was probably drunk at that meeting.

And so over the next couple shows, Chris started getting more and more hammered before each time we'd go out there, and sometimes he'd clearly be *on something*, you know? Like, sometimes he'd be all coked up, and sometimes he'd be sort of zonked out and eventually, like, Trick and I both decided to call Chris's wife, because, I mean, we weren't even sure if she knew what was going on with him, you know, and so we were both just sort of like, this is out of our depth. We need to bring in the big guns. And so we called up Deborah and we were like: Yo, Debbie, Chris is out of control, you gotta come down here.

And, looking back on it, that was probably the worst possible decision we could've made. LOL. Once Debbie got on the bus, that's when shit really hit the fan, because like, apparently she was itching to get back to her glory days too, and so the two of them just started enabling each other like crazy. If I had paid a little more attention to that part of the Thunderbums story—like, if I had read through some of the biographies or watched some of the documentaries—I probably would've known that what we were doing was stupid, but at the time it felt like: If anyone can slow Chris down, it's his wife.

And, you know, the tour basically came to a screeching halt when we were playing a show in Tampa, and Chris was late for the sound check again—this had been happening pretty much the entire time we were on the road—and at this point, like, me and Trick were fucking fed up with it, you know? We were at the end of our rope. And so I was just like: Whatever, I'm *going* to the fucking hotel and I'm *getting* that motherfucker and I'm *bringing* him to sound check. LOL. I was becoming a pretty angry person on that tour.

And so I go to the hotel, and like, I knock on Chris's door, and obviously there's no answer, so I call downstairs to the front desk, and I'm like: I need you to come unlock this shit. And they resisted a bit, but I was like: I paid for these rooms, they're all technically my rooms, open it. And they did. And I went inside, and Chris's room was just a mess—I mean, every place we stayed, Chris and Debbie would just trash it completely. It was really disrespectful. There were bottles all over the place, and like, fast-food wrappers, and pills, and I think Chris must have peed on the couch, because the whole place smelled like piss—and the whole time I was in there, I was calling out like: CHRIS? DEBBIE? WAKE UP, GUYS! IT'S TIME

FOR SOUND CHECK! But I wasn't getting any answer. And so, finally, I made my way into the bathroom, and at first I didn't see them in there, but then I finally looked down at the floor, and I saw the two of them, like, slumped over on top of each other, leaning up against the shower, passed out with needles in their fucking arms.

And that's when I decided to pull the plug. I called an ambulance and had them rushed to the hospital, and I checked them into a rehab facility, and I called Chris's assistant to make sure the kids were being taken care of, and Trick and I just played the rest of the shows without him. We just kicked Chris off the tour. I mean, we were getting toward the end of the American leg anyway, so most of the people we were gonna be playing for at that point didn't really give a shit about Chris—you know, he wasn't that big of a deal in *Japan*—but the whole thing was just really fucking harrowing.

And I guess Chris still sort of blames me for all of it. Like, I guess he still has some sort of deep resentment toward me, because I disturbed his peaceful retirement and I woke up this sleeping devil and brought him back out into the limelight, but, like, how the fuck was I supposed to know, you know? How the fuck was I supposed to predict that Chris would turn into a monster? I read in an interview he did somewhere that he wishes he'd never recorded *Roses and Mud* in the first place because it gave me all of this respect and credibility, and like, all it did for him was just fuck up his plan of getting out of the game before he became an embarrassment. And he's not totally wrong about all that, but that shit is on *him*, you know? You can't go around blaming other people for your shortcomings. If you do that, you're never gonna actually look at yourself in the mirror and be like: What's *going on* with me? Who AM I?

But I don't know. Maybe there's just something wrong with that whole generation. Like, maybe something really fucked up was happening with Chris and my dad and all of those people when they were growing up. I mean, my mom and Bob turned out okay, I guess, so it's not like EVERYBODY that age is fucked up, but maybe something really crazy was happening in the universe at the time when they were born. Like, maybe a whole fucking galaxy got destroyed like, a million light-years away, and so everyone who was born around that time got affected in some crazy way and they don't even know it. I don't know. I'd have to ask Bob how something like that would even work.

#48—Right torso. This is my baby brother's birth date next to a bowl of spaghetti. That's his favorite food right now.

#36—Left chest. This is the plasma gun you get once you reach level 37 in *Urban Warrior*. I know it seems silly, but if you play *U.W.*, you know: That's a HUGE fucking moment.

#13—Upper left cheek. This little guy is modeled after the necklace my mom made for me. Optimus was telling me that unless the person who's asking for it is famous or a criminal—like, unless Optimus is pretty confident they won't ever have to go on a job interview again—he won't do any tattoos above the shirt collar. Apparently, the only people who are allowed to have face tattoos are celebrities and gangsters. LOL.

#60—Right shoulder. This is Curt, Patrick, and Mo as the Three Stooges. It was Mo's idea.

#74—Lower left leg. BEMYBABY1567. This was my gamer tag before I had to change it. I wanted it to just be BEMYBABY, but that was already taken.

Get this:

Mandy just told me she's quitting music.

Seriously!

I don't know if it's public yet, so I'll check with her before I publish anything, but we had lunch yesterday in Chicago, and apparently, over the last couple months, she's been studying with a bunch of tutors and taking the SAT, and she applied to a bunch of different colleges, and she just found out that she got into a bunch of them. She was only in Chicago because she got into a bunch of schools there and she was going to all these admitted students events.

When I talked to her about it, she sounded so *relieved*, you know? I've always kind of felt with Mandy like there was this giant *weight* on her—like there was some deep sadness or like there was something she was holding down in the bottom of her stomach—but this was the first time I talked to her where like, all of that was gone, you know? She felt a thousand pounds lighter.

I asked her if she thought she would get back into the game once she was done with school, and she was like: I don't know. We'll see what happens.

Obviously, like, her manager is freaking out and her label is freaking out, and they're telling her it's this enormous mistake and that if she drops out entirely for four years, it's gonna be really hard for her to get back into it, but Mandy just doesn't give a fuck.

She was just like: That's literally the farthest thing from my mind right now. LOL.

And I really didn't want to be this guy—I support Mandy one hundred percent in whatever she thinks is right for her life—but I just couldn't help saying to her, like: You realize no matter what school you go to, no matter how hard you try to get out of the game, people are gonna be following you around everywhere you go and asking for your autograph and taking pictures of you in class, right?

And Mandy was like: Maybe for the first semester or two. They'll get over it eventually.

And I was like: But what about your roommate? What if she's some crazy person, and you wake up in the middle of the night and she's just like, *staring* at you, you know? Or live-streaming you sleeping?

And Mandy was like: I'm sure whatever she's studying will be more interesting than me.

And I was like: But you realize that whatever you end up doing, whatever kind of life you try to lead, to most people in the world, you're always just gonna be Mandy, right?

And Mandy was like: Most people in the world live on less than two dollars and fifty cents a day. They don't give a shit who "Mandy" is.

And I was like: But a LOT of people do.

And Mandy was like: No. They've been TOLD they do. They've CONVINCED themselves that they do. But the only reason they care about "Mandy" is that the rest of their world is falling apart. "Mandy" is the last little corner of public space where everything appears to be operating normally. "Mandy" is the last little broom closet in the whole exploding factory where people can go and pretend like everything's all right. But everything's not all right. Everything is definitely not all right.

And I was like: Still, it'd be a shame if you quit.

And Mandy just laughed at me, and she was like: *Why?*

And I was like: Because you can SING. You can *really* sing.

And Mandy was like: *Everybody* can sing. That's the beauty of it.

And I was like: I *know*, LOL, but not like *you*.

And Mandy got this look on her face, and for a second, it looked like she was gonna say something, but then she just took out her phone. I didn't really know what she was doing, but she started playing me this sort of amazing recording of this German boys' choir from ten years ago. She didn't say anything to introduce it or set it up: She just found the recording on her phone and pressed play. And they were singing this very traditional, like, very beautiful version of "Silent Night"—you know, except in German it's called "Stille Nacht"—and the whole song was kind of beautiful and amazing, but then in the middle, like, on the second verse, there was this one kid who did a solo—he sounded like he was really young, like, maybe ten or twelve or whatever—and his voice was like, the most amazing thing I had ever heard. I mean, seriously, it was the most delicate and controlled and precise and overpowering thing in the world. And this kid was such a *musician*, you know? Like, he wasn't just talented: He had such complete control over his instrument. He was so *egoless* about it. He was just doing exactly what needed to be done for the song.

And the song finished, and I looked at Mandy, and I was like: Who *was* that kid?

And Mandy looked up at me, and she had tears in her eyes, and she said: That was one of the brothers who carried out the attacks in Berlin. His mother showed it to me when I went to go visit her.

And I was like: Was that the one they captured?

And Mandy shook her head and said: No. That was the one they killed.

Here's the latest from Oddvar:

Yesterday, on the bus, I was checking my emails, and he messaged me being like: Please let me know when I can see you in person during your tour dates in Europe. I have something important I'd like to discuss with you.

And I wrote him back being like: Yo, Oddvar, how are you? What's going on? Is the vault okay?

And Oddvar was like: I need to talk to you. I'll meet you anywhere that is convenient. I hope you are doing well.

And I was like: Listen, man, I'm gonna be in the States for the next week and then when we hit Europe, it's gonna be really quick—like, just a stop in Barcelona and then a stop in Salerno—so I don't know that I'm really gonna have time to hang. Can you just email me?

And Oddvar was like: Barcelona or Salerno is fine. I'll meet you anywhere.

And I was like: Okay, well, let me hit you up when I'm heading over there and we can try to coordinate.

And Oddvar was like: Yes. Wonderful. I look forward to seeing you.

And I was like: Oddvar, what's going on with the vault? You never answered my question.

And Oddvar was like: The vault is being repaired, but it doesn't matter. I'll see you soon.

And then he just signed off.

What does he mean it doesn't matter?

Meanwhile, there's been a little bit of drama with the TV show. I flew back into L.A. for a day to see the screening of the first few episodes—like, before the premiere, you know, the producers were just screening it for my mom and Bob and me and the network executives—and it turns out that instead of being about Bob, most of the show is about my mom. LOL.

She has this group of friends she's been hanging out with since we first moved out to L.A., and they're all sort of these hilarious women in their forties and fifties who like to have drinks together and talk shit about their kids and their jobs and their husbands, and, you know, some of them are actresses and some of them are married to athletes, and they're all sort of brutally honest with each other, like, they say stuff to each other that you're really not supposed to say, but then they've also really got each other's backs, you know? Like, they're all sort of ride or die. And I've known all these women for years, and I've always thought they were sort of amazing, and, apparently, so did the producers of *The Winstocks*, because they structured the whole season around them. They weren't planning to, obviously, but I guess once they started filming, it became clear that they were a gold mine of content, and so the show has sort of ended up becoming a chronicle of their friendship. There's this whole episode where my mom's friend Carol goes to visit her son in rehab, and like, my mom drives her there and they get Burger King afterward and cry together in the parking lot, and there's this episode where Lisa sets up a dating profile after she gets divorced, and my mom is just really mean to her about how she's trying to use pictures from when she was twenty years younger, and they all sort of go through Lisa's matches together and sort them into different categories of fuckability, and it's all kind of irreverent and fun, but it's also really touching, you know? There's a lot of heart, a lot of feels. And there's a *little bit* about Bob— he pops up every once in a while to say something or play with Lenny in the background—and there's a bunch of stuff about my mom's jewelry company and how she's trying to expand the business and get celebrities to wear her pieces at events and stuff, but, for the most part, it's just about these friendships. Bob is sort of a peripheral character.

And the screening fucking killed—I mean, I thought it was amazing, and my mom was having the time of her life, and every single executive was laughing their ass off and crying and congratulating the producers when it was done—but I could tell that Bob wasn't having it. He was standing in the corner when it was over kind of sulking and sipping his drink, and he just looked really pissed off, you know? He was trying to hold it together, but it was like his whole vibe was *heavy*. He was a black hole. And I went up to him, and I was like: How are you feeling, man? What did you think? And Bob just kind of stood there for a while, and then he was like: It's fine. They all seem happy. And I was like: You didn't like it at all? And Bob was like: Who cares if I liked it? And I was like: *Bob*. Come on. You have to at least admit that it's really cool for my mom. And Bob was like: Sure. Good for her. And I was like: *Dude*. What the fuck? And Bob was like: What? What do you want to hear from me? And I was like: You don't think she comes off looking amazing? You don't think it'll be great for her business? And Bob just looked at me with all this *venom* in his face, and he was like: Who cares about her fucking *business*? And then he just walked away.

And I stood there feeling really angry for a moment—I mean, what the fuck, you know?—but then I just looked over at my mom, and she was being fawned over by all these executives, and they were saying all this insane shit to her about how well the show was gonna do and how much they all loved her, and it was like she didn't even notice that Bob was being shitty. It was like she didn't even care. She was just brimming with all this confidence.

And, honestly, in that moment, I was just so proud of her that I was like: Who cares about *Bob*? I just thought she looked so absolutely dope, you know? It was really next-level.

. . .

I don't know how, but news got out that Mandy got into all these colleges—I guess some people in the admissions offices must've leaked it?—and so now there's all this speculation about where she's gonna go.

I'm not totally surprised, but a lot of people are being really shitty about the whole thing. I mean, Mandy got into some pretty serious places—like, we're talking about some of the best schools in the country—and so naturally all of these kids who *didn't* get in are like: How the fuck did *this* idiot get in there? It's probably just because she's *famous.*

And it's like: Sure, I wouldn't put it past some of these places to just let Mandy in because it would be really dope for them if she went there and it would give them all this free publicity, but like, Mandy fucking *deserved* to get into those schools. Like, I basically annoyed the shit out of Mandy until she told me what she got on her SATs, and I looked up what her score meant on my phone, and it was like: Whoa. Okay. I mean, we're talking genius level. Seriously. And, meanwhile, all these idiot kids are posting shit like: If Mandy goes to my school, I might as well burn my diploma because it means *nothing.* I mean, obviously that's not *everybody*—like, obviously, there are some really cool, like, really amazing kids who are being like: Mandy! Choose us! We love you!—but there were a few things I saw online that were just really mean-spirited, and it's like: Why WOULDN'T you want to go to school with Mandy? You would be LUCKY to share the same space with her.

I texted her today when I was looking at all this shit

being like: Yo, are you okay? A lot of nasty shit's being said about you.

And Mandy was like: Oh, is there? She hadn't even heard about it.

I explained to her what people were saying, and I was like: Fuck these people, man. They're just jealous. And Mandy didn't even say anything. She just sent me this article with the headline: "Greenland Is Burning." And I clicked on it, and it was about how, for the first time ever, Greenland has been having these uncontrollable forest fires because the permafrost that used to cover the ground there has melted away, and now they're finding out that what's been underneath it this whole time is *peat*—basically, just like, pure decayed vegetable matter: pure CO_2. According to the article, the fires have been burning for weeks, and no one knows how to put them out. Instead of spreading around like regular wildfires, they just burn straight into the ground.

I think I finally figured out the dad moment in the video game, by the way.

I was driving through Iowa with Deez this afternoon—he hopped on the tour for a few nights in Chicago and Cincinnati, and now we're heading to a show in Des Moines before we hop on a plane again and chill out for a few days in L.A.—and Deez was getting blazed as we were passing through this giant field of cows—like, legitimately, thousands of cows on either side of the highway—and I was looking out the window, and it dawned on me:

I *know* what would've happened if I found my dad before he killed himself.

I *know* what would've happened if I busted down the door to the old house and found him in my room with the gun in his mouth and his finger on the trigger.

I *know* what would've happened if I screamed: Dad, stop! Or if I pulled out my guitar and started to play something for him.

I *know*.

He would've looked at me, and he would've smiled, and he would've gone ahead and pulled the trigger anyway.

I mean, actually, me being there might've made the whole thing better for him—it might've made the gesture even more complete.

And so there's really no point in imagining the whole scenario.

Actually, I'm kind of starting to doubt the whole video game if I'm being honest. Not just because it keeps getting more and more expensive and not just because it's probably gonna look like shit when it's finished, but I guess it's just starting to feel ridiculous to imagine any sort of alternative to the way things are. I've just started to feel like maybe everyone could only ever be exactly who they turned out to be. Maybe that's just some law of the universe.

I was always gonna be me, and you were always gonna be you, and my dad was always gonna be my dad, and Mandy was always gonna be Mandy, and the guys who did that shit at her concert were always gonna be the guys who did that shit at her concert, and my mom was always gonna be my mom, and Bob was always gonna be Bob, and Patrick and Curt and Mo were always gonna be Patrick and Curt and Mo, and Deez was always gonna be Deez, and Trick was always gonna be Trick, and Chris Jeffries was always gonna be Chris Jeffries, and Oddvar was always gonna be Oddvar.

        My second to last day in L.A., he just shows up at my house.

We had just finished the state-by-state leg of the tour—I was back for a few days to recharge and get my bearings before we got on the plane again—and I guess Oddvar must've known I'd be taking a few days off, because he shows up at the gate in a taxi, and he's like: Hi! I'm in Los Angeles now! Can I come in?

And I was just like: Whoa, Oddvar. What the fuck?

Patrick and Mo were not having it. They were just immediately like: *No.* They saw the taxi pull up at the gate on the security camera and they were like: What the fuck is this? What is he doing here? And they *know* Oddvar, you know, like, they *like* Oddvar, but the second they smell trouble or like, the second they get a whiff of something that's a little out of the ordinary, they're just like: Nope. This isn't how you do this.

Because you gotta understand, like: You can't just *show up* at my house. I know that makes me seem like a dick or whatever, but like, I'm not just your *buddy* where you can roll up at my front door and surprise me and drop in on me unannounced. That's kind of a loaded situation to put me in. You've gotta at least text me in advance or we have to have talked about it a little bit just so that I can let the guys know and nobody goes into crisis mode.

But, you know, I heard the phone ring from the gate and I went and looked at the security camera and I saw that it was Oddvar, and I was like: What the fuck is HE doing here? So I talked to the guys, and I was like: Let me at least talk to him. Let me see what's up.

I asked him over the intercom like: What are you doing at my house, Oddvar? What's going on? I thought I was seeing you in Europe?

And Oddvar was just like: I know! I'm sorry, but I couldn't wait! I quit working at the seed vault! I wanted to come see you!

And I was like: You *quit* working at the seed vault?

And Oddvar was like: Yes! It's very exciting!

And I was like: Why did you do that?

And Oddvar was like: Let me come in! I'll tell you all about it!

And I looked at Patrick and Mo and they were shaking their heads like: No, man. No fucking way. But, you know, it's *Oddvar.* I mean, he named a fucking *seed* after me. I wasn't gonna leave him out on the street. I opened up the gate for him, and his taxi dropped him off at the front door, and we all went to go meet him in the entryway.

And Oddvar comes in, and he looks fucking *weird,* you know? I mean, he's not dressed weird or anything—actually, if anything, he was dressed super WELL. Like, he sort of looked crisp and clean in this very L.A. way, like he could've been any of those guys walking around Rodeo Drive—but something about him, something about his whole vibe was just *off.* I mean, he was wearing a pair of *sunglasses*, you know? Like, *really nice sunglasses*. And this is *Oddvar* we're talking about. Usually, he just looks like a grad student.

All the other times when I saw him, something I always really loved about Oddvar was that he was so chill, you know what I mean? Like, he sort of treated me like a scientist, or like, he always seemed to have this *distance*, this *remove*. But now that he was in my house, like, now that he was in my world, it was like ALL of that was gone. He was acting like a totally different person. Everything was fucking magical to him. He was moving through the house like I had touched every object with fairy stardust or like he was walking through an enchanted forest. And I offered him a sparkling water—like, just a normal fucking sparkling water—and he accepted it like: Wow, amazing. Wow. I mean, he really wasn't doing himself any favors in terms of putting Patrick and Mo at ease.

And after a while of giving him a tour of my place—I showed him the studio, which he totally lost his shit over, and the gym, and the pool, and he was drooling over everything, like, treating me like I was the president or something giving him a tour of the White House—I finally asked him, like: Yo, Oddvar, what do you mean you quit working at the seed vault?

And Oddvar just gets this big smile on his face, and he goes, like, rapid fire: It was so stupid! LOL. What was I thinking! That place was never gonna work. You can't save the world with a bunch of fucking SEEDS.

And I was like: Oddvar, what are you talking about? The seed vault has been your whole life.

And he was like: I know! So STUPID! But I've still got

time to do something worthwhile! I've still got time to turn it around!

And I was like: Is this all just because of the flood? I thought you said they were going to fix it?

And Oddvar was like: Sure, yes, they "fixed it." *So what?* How long until it floods again? How long until the next crisis? I'm done being an idiot. What kind of life is it to collect seeds in the middle of a mountain?

And I was like: Oddvar, whoa, but come on, you can't just give up like that.

And Oddvar was like: I'm not giving up! Not in the least! I'm not giving up on the future. I've just realized that even at its best, the seed vault was always theoretical. Meanwhile, you're *right here*! And I could've lost you! The whole world could've lost you!

And I was like: Oddvar, I told you, it's fine. I forgive you.

And Oddvar was like: I know. I know. Your kindness and generosity astound me. But I'm done with that chapter of my life. There's nothing you could do or say to convince me otherwise. When the flood happened, I was plunged into a deep depression. I couldn't leave my room for days. I looked out my window at the ice and thought: Why not just walk out there and keep walking? Why not leave the vault with no clothes and no supplies and go meet Nature face-to-face to see how much she cares about my love for her? What will it be *worth* to her that I've spent my life in service of her preservation? What will it be *worth* to her that I've invested so much in the preservation of my species? I thought about all the seeds I had cataloged, all the days and nights I had spent printing out labels and sorting boxes, all the grant applications I'd filled out, all the phone calls I'd made, all the emails I'd sent back and forth with all the other seed vaults around the world, and I realized that it all amounted to *nothing*. It was all just a little *club*, a little *game* that a few sad idiots were playing to keep themselves occupied in the cold. It was a lie we had all told ourselves so that we could feel like we had some agency against the vast, uncaring power of the Universe. What could be more arrogant than to think you could bargain with Nature? Who could be so foolish? And then I remembered: This isn't all I have. This isn't the sum of who I am. I thought my work at the seed vault was my deepest connection with humanity, but in fact, it was my other life, what I had thought of before as my *secondary* life, where I had been harboring my REAL humanity. I'm a FAN. I'm *your biggest* fan. And, in a way, that makes me the biggest fan of *humanity itself.* I remembered the way I felt when I first heard "Don't Look Back" all those years ago, and I realized that as long as I still had your voice, as long as humanity could still foster something as powerful and beautiful as your talent, there was still something meaningful that I could do. There was still some way that I could be useful to my fellow man. And so I resolved right then and there to begin my new life and move to Los Angeles.

And I was like: You're *moving* here?

And he was like: Yes! Most of my things are still in Spitsbergen, but this is where I was meant to be! This is where I belong!

And I was like: Oddvar, what are you even gonna DO here?

And Oddvar was like: Well, actually, that's what I wanted to come talk to you about . . .

And then he just launched into this crazy monologue about how he wanted to come work for me. Like, he started rattling off all of these ideas he had for my career, and he pulled out his *own* tattoo map of my body—like, he KNEW we hired a graphic designer to draw one up. I *talked* to him about it a bunch of times—but for whatever reason, he spent all this time drawing up his own super-detailed diagram, and, like, it looked *fine*, I guess, but it was still like: Why did you waste all your time doing this, you know? What do you want ME to do with it?

And the craziest part, I mean, the part that actually kind of pissed me off was that like, Oddvar started telling me all his ideas for my fourth album. He was just like: Listen, I've been thinking a lot about it, and I know you've been having trouble figuring out what the next album's gonna be, so here are all my ideas, and he started listing people he thought I should work with and songs he thought I should sample and potential names for the album, and it was just like: What the fuck is going on with you? I mean, obviously I haven't told Oddvar that it's a video game, but still, it's like, Oddvar never just launches in with his two cents like that. It was really uncharacteristic.

And so I was just like: Listen, Oddvar, this is all a little heavy. I wish you would've warned me about all this in an email or something before you made your decision.

And Oddvar was like: Of course. Of course. Take your time. But just know that when you're ready, I'll be here. I am your faithful servant for life. You're my guardian angel.

And so we hung out for a bit more at the house—I didn't really know what to say to him, so we mostly just like, sat there on the couch, and he would smile at me and then look around and go: Wow. Wow—and then later that night, I took him out on the town.

I mean, honestly, I just wanted to chill while I was in L.A., you know? Like, I really could've used that time to decompress and relax and just be alone and think about the book—I have to submit a draft to the publishers soon, so I wasn't really planning on going out and seeing people at all—but the vibe at home with Oddvar just hanging around on my couch, being a total fucking freak about everything and foaming at the mouth, was kind of freaking me out, and I figured if we at least got out of the house, maybe it'd get a little better. So I said to him, like: Yo, let's get out of here. Let's go eat some sushi and check out a club or two. And Oddvar was like: Wow, amazing! A truly authentic L.A. experience! And so I called up a few people to see if they wanted to meet up with us, and we ended up getting together with Z Bunny and a few people from his crew.

And the whole time we were out, Oddvar was being *super* weird with everybody. It was like everything was the coolest thing he had ever seen. He was laughing WAY too hard at people's jokes, and like, taking selfies with everybody the whole time, and asking Z about all of his tattoos, and asking all of Z's crew like: And what do YOU do? And what do YOU do? And he was telling anyone who would listen about how fucking stupid the seed vault was and what an idiot he had been to devote his life to it and how L.A. was the only sane place on Earth, and I even had to tap him on the shoulder a few times and be like: Yo, man, chill. Calm down a little bit.

And then in the club, he just got *super-wasted*. Like, he was paying for everybody's drinks—I kept telling him he didn't have to since he was my guest, but he was like: No, no, it's all on me. I love this place! I love it!—and he was putting away like, five, six, maybe seven drinks within the first HOUR that we were there. I didn't even know he LIKED drinking *at all*, you know, but here he was like, trying to shut the bar down.

And at a certain point, like, the club started playing "Love Hug"—you know, that song I made with Z a few years ago—and Oddvar just lost his shit. Like, he was treating it like it was the biggest coincidence in the world, and it was just like: Dude, this shit happens *all the time*. It's not that big of a deal. But Oddvar was singing along to it and trying to dance with me and get me to sing along with it, and like, he was rapping all the words to Z's part, and people were looking at him like: WTF? Patrick and Mo were watching him like HAWKS, you know? They just wanted to get rid of him.

And so when it came time for everyone to go home, me and Patrick and Mo had this little conference about what to do with Oddvar, and I mean, it wasn't THAT late, but I think Z and his crew were kind of weirded out by the whole situation, and I was pretty tired, because we had just been grinding for so many weeks in a row, and so Patrick and Mo were like: Let's go. Oddvar can find his own way home. And I looked over at Oddvar, and he was like, dancing by himself, like, wobbling all over the place, starting on his ninth or tenth drink, and I was just like: Guys, dude is WASTED. I don't even know if he has a place to stay tonight. Let's just put him up in the guesthouse.

And Patrick got *pissed*. I mean, literally, I could see the veins popping out of his forehead. I've never seen him so angry at me before. He was just like: You've got to be fucking kidding me.

And I was like: Dude, we can't just LEAVE him here. He doesn't know anybody in L.A.

And Patrick was like: He's a grown man. He can figure it out.

And I was like: Come on, man. He hosted us on a fucking *island* in the middle of nowhere. The least we can do is make sure he doesn't choke on his own vomit.

And Patrick was like: The guy is bad vibes. We need to get rid of him. Now.

And I was like: Patrick, it's *Oddvar*.

And Patrick was like: Does that *look* like fucking Oddvar to you?

And we looked over at him, and he was like, drunkenly trying to do the Macarena or something in the middle of the dance floor, and we were both just sort of like: Fuck, man. What's going ON here?

And during the whole car ride home, Oddvar was just looking out the window at L.A. being like: This is the PLACE! This is the PLACE! Even when we were stopped at a red light in front of a gas station, Oddvar was just like: YES! I love it!

And back home, like, I wanted to make sure he got back to his room okay, you know, since he was sort of tripping around all over the place, and so me and the guys put our arms around him and got him into the guesthouse, and like, we sat him down on the bed, and I was like: You okay, Oddvar? You need some water?

And Oddvar was like: I'm amazing. Never been better. Thank you. Thank you.

And I was like: All right, man. Good night. Get some rest.

And Oddvar was like: Thank you for existing. Thank you for your life.

And I was like: Sleep tight, man. Go to bed.

And I started to leave, but Oddvar was like: Wait! Wait. I need to tell you something.

And I was like: What's up, Oddvar? What's going on?

And Oddvar was like: Just you. I just want to tell you.

And I was like: Patrick and Mo can't hear it?

And Oddvar was like: No! No. Just you!

And I looked at Patrick and Mo, and they both just looked at me like: No fucking way. We're not moving an inch. And so I looked back at Oddvar, and I was like: Why don't you just tell me tomorrow, okay?

And Oddvar sort of slurred-shouted something.

And I was like: Huh? I couldn't hear you.

And Oddvar was like: I love you.

And I was like: I love you too, man. Good night.

And Oddvar was like: I *love* you. I *really* love you.

And I was, like: Okay, man, that's dope. Go to bed.

And Oddvar was like: Be my baby . . .

And I was like: What?

And Oddvar grabbed my arm, and he was like: Kiss me!

And already the guys were rushing over to pull him off of me, but Oddvar was like, grabbing my shoulders and trying to bring me down to him on the bed—he was drunk as hell, but he had all this *strength*, you know? It was like he was possessed by something—and he was just like: Kiss me! Kiss me!

And I was like: Oddvar! What the fuck? Let go of me!

And his face looked so desperate, you know? Like, there was so much sadness in it, but there was also this sort of *hunger*. And he was just like: Kiss me. Kiss me.

And Patrick and Mo started grabbing him really roughly to get him off of me, and I was immediately like: Guys! Take it easy! Don't hurt him!

And Oddvar was like: Kiss me! Please! Kiss me!

And Patrick was ready to throw down—like, he had his fist cocked back and he was ready to smash Oddvar's face in—but I was like: Patrick! Chill! It's okay!

And so Patrick just threw him down on the mattress, like, really hard, and immediately, Oddvar started throwing up all over the side of the bed.

It got all over my shoes and Patrick's shoes and Mo's shirt, and we were all just like: Fuck, man! What the fuck?

And right when he was done, like, right after the last little bits of it came out of his mouth, Oddvar just cocked his head back onto the pillow and fell asleep. He was just like: PLOP, and, instantly, he was out.

And Patrick was like: I'm gonna wake this mother-fucker up right now and throw him out on the street. I mean, seriously, Patrick was *pissed*. He was about to do some *military* shit.

But I was like: Patrick, it's fine, man. Let him sleep. The housekeepers will clean this up in the morning.

And so Patrick just kind of threw his hands up in the

air and left the room. He didn't even say good night to me or anything.

And I looked at Oddvar for a second—he was lying there snoring and shit, and for the first time all night, he looked kind of peaceful, you know? Like, he almost kind of looked like his old self—but then he started humming "Love Hug" in his sleep, and so I left the room.

And the next day when I woke up and went to go check on him, he was gone. No note, no apology, nothing. He had cleaned up all the vomit and like, made the bed, and gathered up all his shit, and he was out of there. It was like he was never there in the first place.

And I sent him an email being like: What the fuck, man? Where'd you go?

But I haven't heard anything back from him.

#56—Left lower stomach. This is the face of that woman who tried to kill me in Australia. For the longest time, I kept thinking I was seeing her all over the place, you know? Like, I'd think she was gonna turn up on the street in L.A. or like, show up at a concert in Oklahoma, and so I just thought like, if I just put her on my body, at least she'll always be there with me. There will be nothing left to fear. Sometimes, I just think about that woman's life. For whatever reason, I imagine that it's super-fucking-normal. Like, I bet she's a school nurse or something. I bet her family doesn't have any clue what she tried to do to me. I didn't have a picture of her or anything, so I just described her face as best as I could remember it to Optimus, and he tatted it as I went along. It was like a police sketch or something, except it was in black ink and it was on my stomach. That's where she almost cut me.

#38—Right ankle. This is Jessie, the little Pomeranian we used to have in St. James. My parents got her around the time that I was born, and she died when I was like, six or seven, I think. My dad accidentally closed the garage door on her one day, and we were all SO sad. LOL.

#80—Right forearm. Each one of these tally marks represents a million views on that first video we uploaded of me singing the national anthem. Since it's just a bunch of fucking straight lines, I've actually been doing these myself, but every time I see Optimus, he tells me what a bad job I'm doing. He's like: How could you fuck up a *straight line*, bro? But I'm like: Dude, what are you *talking* about? These look fine.

The day after all the shit with Oddvar, I threw a little party at my place celebrating Mandy getting into college.

It was the Fourth of July, so I was planning on having a little get-together anyway, but I was feeling really proud of her, you know, and I knew she wasn't gonna do anything for herself, so I turned it into a college acceptance party instead.

And we didn't have a chef or anything—it was just me and Bob on the grill—and my mom was there, and Lenny, and Curt and Mo and Patrick and Gloria and Amelia, and Deez and Trick, and Kelly, and some of Mandy's brothers and their kids, and all of my mom's friends, and the camera crew, and we just sort of like, had some beers and set up the slip-and-slide in the backyard and played some music and celebrated.

Bob seemed like he had chilled out a little bit since the show premiered. He was still kind of mad for a while after that screening, and my mom was saying he was still being shitty around the house, but then when *The Winstocks* actually came out a few weeks ago and it had the kind of impact that it had and it brought in all the numbers that it did, I think Bob just sort of realized that even if the show didn't turn out the way he had imagined it, it was still gonna be this *cultural force,* you know, and he could either be a part of it or not. If the point was to use the format of a reality show to connect with people and get into their lives, *The Winstocks* was definitely doing that, and so if Bob wanted to ride that wave in any capacity, he was gonna have to chill the fuck out and start being more supportive of my mom, because there was no changing the fact that she was at the front of the surfboard: It was all gonna happen with or without him.

He'll still every once in a while try to take control of the show in little ways: like, now that they're filming the second season, whenever the cameras are around, he'll try to get their attention by talking about something really strange or controversial, and he'll try to insert himself into conversations that my mom is having with her friends for no reason—like, he'll go into the kitchen if my mom is in there talking with somebody, and he'll just start *doing the dishes,* you know? Like, Bob never *does the dishes,* but he'll just start doing them so that he can chime in and be included, and he'll try to say all this shit that he thinks will sound interesting, but since it has nothing to do with what anyone's talking about and since it's all kind of forced and awkward, it always ends up just falling flat, and then sometimes one of my mom's friends will look into the camera like: *What the fuck is he talking about?*—but, for the most part, Bob's been keeping his shit together. I mean, honestly, I'm a little worried that when they start editing the second season, Bob's gonna end up looking like this *crazy person*, you know? Or like, some really annoying *roommate* who's always hanging around in the background and won't shut up. But whatever. He can handle it. As long as he's not fucking with my mom's vibe, I'm good. He pretends that he doesn't really care about the show and that he was never that invested to begin with, and my mom pretends that she believes him, and that honestly seems to be working for everybody, so I'm not gonna rock the boat.

The show's already totally changed the game for her just in terms of her business and her image and all the different opportunities it's been opening up. She's been going on talk shows and getting all these orders online for her stuff and getting profiled in magazines, and, for the first time since she was thrust into the spotlight however many years ago, it feels like she's being looked at for *her*, you know, for something *she's* doing for *herself*, so she's honestly just been kind of *busy*. She kind of seems like she's too busy to really think about Bob *at all*. She never wants to talk about it. And, so far at least, Bob's been able to keep his shit under control to the extent that it's not blowing up in anyone's face, so I guess that's all you can ask for. I mean, I don't know. It's kind of insane how low the bar has been set when it comes to the behavior I'm calling acceptable—like, my mom is supposed to be *thrilled* that Bob is basically doing the bare minimum of not completely ruining a good thing that's happening *in spite of him*—but, as long as my mom is fine with the system they've set up for themselves, who am I to say it's unsustainable? I've definitely seen worse. She's definitely been inside worse.

I guess I'm just kind of surprised, you know, that it's even *possible* for someone like Bob to be like this. I mean, I know that probably sounds hilarious to a lot of people, like, especially the people who have been wary of Bob from the start—I'm sure for them, it's just like: Yeah, this is what guys like Bob *do*. This is who they *are*—but I guess I'm just really confused about how you can make it through life this long and have a whole *career* as a *writer* and a *thinker* and still be such a little bitch. LOL. Like, I used to think it was kind of annoying when people would say that Bob was such a *man*, you know, that all the things he was saying could only be said by a *man* whose life had been just like Bob's—I used to just kind of be like: Yeah, okay, sure, I mean, you're right, but that's not the *point*. What about all the other stuff? What about the *interesting* stuff?—but now when I look at Bob, it's really hard to see anything other than a little rich boy who can't even be proud of his *wife*. I mean, it's actually fucking pathetic. I've been trying to think back to all the things he's written that have actually changed my life, or like, all the conversations we've had that have been sort of mind-blowing or next-level, and it's impossible to get it out of my mind that he's losing his shit right now over a *reality show*. Like, that's actually what he's doing. He actually can't handle the fact that my mom *stole The Winstocks from him*. And, meanwhile, Bob's whole thing is about *truth*, you know— his whole MO is about being really honest with ourselves and investigating all the ways that we're committed to bullshit and all the ways we're prevented from being free—but it's almost like he's never actually taken a minute and been like: What kind of bullshit am *I* committed to? What kind of weakness is actually holding *me* back? He *says* he does: like, in all his books, he says that he's been so ruthless with himself, so unsparing. He says that his entire philosophy is a process of throwing out past selves until he arrives at a new one. But what does that all amount to if it ends up looking like *this*? It's not even disappointing, you know? It's just really, really sad. And more than that, it's *boring*.

I think that's probably why Bob's never dealt with it: because he thinks he's entitled to only think about interesting things. He's assumed for all the decades he's been alive that if something is boring, that must mean it's not worth thinking about. And I bet whenever anyone would bring it up with him, he would just be like: This is *boring*. Why can't we talk about *something else*? I mean, actually, I *know* he would do that. He used to do that shit to Mandy back in the day whenever she would ask him why he said that thing about gay people or why he was saying that people like her parents were barely alive or even just why he was being such an asshole to her, you know? And I used to watch the two of them arguing and think: Bob's right. This IS boring. Mandy is making us think about boring things. But the truth is that a *lot* of shit is boring— a lot of really important shit is boring—and if you create a situation for yourself where you're *afraid* of thinking about the boring shit, where you don't even want to look at the boring shit for more than a second because you think that it will make *you* boring, what actually ends up happening is that you *do* become boring. Your worst fear comes true, and it's only happening because you're afraid of it. And at a certain point, that becomes the difference between children and adults, you know? You can say all the crazy shit you want, and you can be the smartest person in the room, but if you're talking to an adult and you haven't dealt with your boring shit, at a certain point, they're gonna be like: Oh. This is a *child*. And then, in their mind, they're gonna be done with you. Or, at the very least, they're gonna put you in a box where they put children who look like adults.

I mean, honestly, that seems to be what Mandy's been doing with Bob. Ever since she had her sort of awakening, she and Bob disagree on like, absolutely everything when it comes to *the world*, but they seem to at least be getting along a lot better and having a good time talking to each other. And for a while, I thought it was because they were finding some common ground, but now I think it's just because Mandy can see that Bob is a child, you know? She's not really *bothered* by him anymore. She can just sort of laugh at him now.

At a certain point during the party, Mandy and I found ourselves alone in the house. I'm saying it like it was an accident, but Mandy sort of tugged at my sleeve and started walking in, and I followed her. And I was thinking like: Whoa, okay, maybe this is starting up again, you know? I mean, there's been something about Mandy that's been like, really *sexy* recently. Or, beyond sexy even: She's just got all of this confidence—like, she's got this AURA around her. Whatever vibe she's on right now is one that I want to get closer to.

So we went down into my studio, and I turned on the lava lamp down there and got us some beers, and Mandy noticed that the video game was open on my computer, and she was like: Whoa, what the fuck is THIS thing? And I was like: Fuck, I can't believe I forgot to close that. My first impulse was to lie about it and keep it a secret—you know, because I've been pretty committed to no one finding out about it until it's done—but then I thought about it for a second, and I was just like: You know what? I'm not even sure I like this thing anymore. I'd actually be really interested to see what Mandy thinks about it. So I said to her: This is the thing I've been working on. You wanna see it?

And Mandy was like: Yes.

So I sat her down in front of the computer, and I told her about the concept of the game a little bit, and I loaded up one of the early demo levels, and I watched her play.

It was the level where you've just arrived in L.A. and you meet Mandy at the head of the label's place in Malibu, and you have to play this, like, little flirting mini-game in order to get with her. It's mostly just little conversation trees—Mandy asks you if you miss St. James, and you have a few options, like, "Nah, not really," or like, "Yes, all the time," or like, "Yeah, but L.A.'s amazing!"— and depending on what you say and depending on what she says like, the flirting either goes really well or it goes really badly. And even if it goes badly, like, the whole time you're there, there are still all these other people at the party who give you boosts here and there and give you extra bonus points whenever it looks like you're about to lose, so you have to be trying really hard if you wanna fuck it up.

And I expected Mandy to kind of think it was cute and like, maybe remember what it was like to be around at that time, you know, remember what it was like to fall in love with me, but instead, at a certain point, she just pushed the keyboard away from herself and looked down at the ground, kind of pissed, and I was like: Whoa, Mandy, what's wrong? You don't like it?

And Mandy was like: We were so young then . . . We weren't even people . . .

And I was like: No. LOL. We were babies.

And Mandy was like: We were child soldiers. We didn't own a single part of ourselves.

And I was like: I guess not. But it really felt like we were in love then, didn't it?

And Mandy was like: So many things felt real that weren't. We were the last people on Earth who would've known the difference.

And there was this silence for a bit, and we both just kind of sat there, and then Mandy looked at the video game for a second, and then she looked back at me, and she was like: Would you quit?

And I was like: Quit what?

And Mandy was like: Being famous.

And I was like: You mean, just like, walk away? Do what you're doing?

And Mandy was like: Yeah.

And I didn't say anything for a while, and then Mandy was like: You think that it'll feel like dying. But it won't. Once you do it, it's as easy as taking off a pair of headphones.

And I still didn't really know what to say, and so Mandy was like: We're still so young. We can still be whoever we want to be.

And I was like: I'm *being* whoever I want to be.

And Mandy was like: *This* is who you want to be? *This?*

And I was like: Yeah.

And Mandy was like: *Why?*

And I was like: Because . . . I'm showing people what it's like to be free.

And Mandy was like: You think you're *free?*

And I was like: Freer than a normal person at least.

And Mandy was like: You are the biggest slave on the planet. You are an advertisement for a fake world. You think you're the CEO, but you're not even on the board. Just because people are staring at you doesn't mean they admire you. They want to *eat* you. And of course they do. They're *starving.* You're the cheap fuel that keeps the whole thing running.

And I was like: You want me to stop being famous? You want me to just become a normal person?

And Mandy was like: You already ARE a normal person. That's all anyone can ever be.

And I was like: Then how come I don't feel like one?

And Mandy was like: You wanna know the difference between a normal person and a famous person?

And I was like: What?

And Mandy was like: A famous person is just a normal person who thinks they exist.

And right then, really loudly, "Be My Baby" started playing on my computer speakers. In the game, if you don't select anything for a while in the conversation trees, it just automatically gets you together with Mandy, and so Mandy and I both looked over at the screen as this cut scene started to play of the two of us walking down to the beach and having our first kiss.

Sitting there with Mandy, watching the two of us kissing in the game and listening to my thirteen-year-old voice doing all this crazy shit on the soundtrack, it was like, all of a sudden, time stopped, and I could see the future.

I saw Mandy, and she was sitting in an office somewhere at some university, and she was a professor, and all over her walls were posters for different talks she had given or different conferences she had organized, and on her shelves were all these books—books she was reading and books she had written—and in the little corner of her office, not hidden or anything, but just not given the front and center placement, there was a picture of her from the *Mobilize* tour. Just a little framed picture—it felt like the kind of thing she'd show her students sometimes when they came in and be like: Look what I used to do. Look who I used to be. And they'd laugh and be like: WHAT? LOL. Or maybe they'd already know about it, but they'd still just be like: Whoa, Professor, you've had the craziest life experience. It was like Mandy was able to have such a sense of humor about it, you know? No anger, no resentment, just: That's life. That's where life can take you.

And even though I could see Mandy so clearly—like, even though Future Mandy was coming in loud and clear—I found myself thinking: What's gonna happen to *me* when I'm that age? Where am *I* gonna be when Mandy's looking like this?

For all the time I'd spent in the video game trying to figure out how I got here—like, trying to think about all the other people I *could've been* if I had made different choices or if I had walked into different situations—I hadn't really spent any time thinking about the person *I was going to be.* I'd thought about whether anyone was gonna be listening to my music a thousand years from now, and I'd thought about how all the stuff I'd *already* done was gonna be remembered or if it was gonna be remembered at all, but I'd never actually thought about what *I* was gonna be like when I was fifty, sixty, seventy years old. And it's like: Why not, you know? Why didn't I try to make a video game about THAT? Was it just because I'd been so locked into the moment, so focused on living in the here and now, that it didn't seem worth my time or my energy? Was there some part of me that didn't think I was gonna make it that far, or that the whole world wasn't gonna make it that far? Or was it actually something deeper? Was it actually that I knew somewhere in the back of my mind that all the work I needed to do, all the stuff I was here for, was happening *right now*—the golden age of me being able to be *this guy*, live *this life*, was happening right at this very instant—and so if I could see what the world had in store for me, I would just be like: Fuck it. What's the point?

But I was feeling kind of . . . I don't know. I guess I was

feeling kind of inspired by how brave Mandy seemed to be these days. I was feeling like if it scared me so much to think about this shit, like, if I was so worried about what I was gonna see when I looked into the crystal ball, that meant I had to do it. And, like, maybe my life was about to unravel. Maybe if I thought about it really hard and I was really honest with myself, I was gonna see something that was so clear and so convincing that I couldn't unsee it.

But I was there, and I was feeling brave, and so I entered into the space of total possibility. I submitted the question to the universe: What's going to happen to me? Who am I going to become?

And the universe answered back with this naked, saggy, tatted old man.

LOL.

Or, I mean, it wasn't exactly like that. It wasn't that simple. I was staring into this giant void—it was like a loading screen in a video game, you know, where you can still sort of walk around as the character but none of the surfaces have loaded and you're just sort of lost in the matrix—and all of a sudden, right in the middle of the void, I saw myself, sixty years in the future, standing there, naked, looking right at me. I still had all my tats—or at least most of them—but I was like, an OLD man, you know? My skin was saggy as shit, and like, I had all those weird splotches that old people have, and some of my tats had faded really badly, and some I had covered up with other tats or like, well, I guess I must've had them removed, and there were all these new tats—so many of them—and I had no idea what most of them signified. There were some that were just dope as shit and that's clearly why I got them—like, there was this one of an alligator on my neck that was like, I mean, I don't know if it was Optimus that did it, but if it was, then he really steps up his game in the future—but most of them clearly had all this deep significance that I just didn't understand yet: It was like looking at hieroglyphics from the future. And it was all a little overwhelming, because like, obviously, I wasn't just focusing on the tats: I was looking at my body, and I was staring into my face, and the future me, the old man me, wasn't smiling or frowning or really doing anything at all. He was just *there*, you know? He was just this *person*. I had clearly stopped working out, and it's not like I looked unhealthy or crazy or anything, but I just looked like an old man: I had a little potbelly, and I had that weird turkey-neck thing that my grandpa had, and it was kind of like when you see paparazzi shots of really old famous people on the beach or on vacation, and they've got no clothes or like, no hairstyle to communicate that they're any different from anyone else, and so it just looks like you snapped a picture of some old biker guy, you know, or like, somebody's dad.

And I didn't know anything about him—like, I didn't know if he was still making music, and I didn't know if he had a family or like, I didn't know if he was sick or healthy—so I asked him, like: Hey, man. How are you doing? What's going on with you?

And the old man just kind of looked at me and didn't say anything.

And I was like: Nice tats, man. When do I get all these?

And the old man just looked at me and didn't say anything.

And I was like: So I live this long? I live long enough to look like you?

And the old man just looked at me and didn't say anything.

And I thought about what my fans would think if they could see right then what I was seeing. What would it mean for them if they knew that this was the end game? How would it affect the way they look at me now? Would they still like it when I posted a picture online? Would they still show up at my concerts and scream their heads off when I did my dance moves? They must all know somewhere in the back of their minds that this is where we're heading, but what would it be like for them to actually SEE it? To actually hold it in their hands?

I noticed that the old man was singing something. He was just like, mouthing it really quietly, and so I listened—I pricked up my ears and really concentrated on what was coming out of his mouth—and even though he sounded like me, like, even though his voice was still undeniably MY voice, I guess just because I was so much older or like, because my voice had gotten really worn down over the years, it just sounded kind of . . . *normal*. Like, it wasn't *bad*—I still sounded like someone who could carry a tune, maybe even like a professional—but the actual quality of the voice, the actual timbre and resonance, were nothing to write home about.

And I listened to the song he was singing, and I realized that it was "The Star-Spangled Banner." LOL. It didn't even really register at first, because the way he was singing it, it was just like he was taking the song at face value, you know? There were no trills, no extra measures, no pyrotechnics—he was just like, *doing the song.* I realized that without all the extras, without all the embellishments and the showmanship, the song actually kind of . . . *sucks.* There's nothing to hold on to in terms of a hook or a melody.

And I tried to think back to the moment when my twelve-year-old self became a superstar. I tried to travel back in time to when my dad and I recorded that video at my desk in St. James. I was there, pulling out every trick in the book, putting all this energy and emotion and ambition into this thing that was probably never meant to be sung like that in the first place, that wasn't even a *song,* really. I tried to connect with the little boy who was putting everything he had into this poem about rockets and bombs and ramparts so that he could prove to the world that he deserved to be where I am now, that the world had no choice but to put him there. And right at the moment when we finished recording, right when my dad pressed the button on the computer and said: That's it, I paused everything and asked myself: Is this the life you imagined? Is this who you thought you would become?

I snapped out of the void—I came back to the real world, back to the studio with Mandy—and she had turned off the computer speakers that were playing "Be My Baby," and she was looking at me like: Where did you just go?

And I told her about everything—the old man, the video, the national anthem—and Mandy listened to me for a minute, and then she was like: Go get your guitar.

And I was like: Okay. And I picked up my acoustic off of the little stand.

And Mandy was like: Play something.

And I was like: What do you want me to play?

And Mandy was like: We're gonna make a new national anthem.

And I was like: Whoa. LOL.

And Mandy was like: It's gotta be catchy, and it's gotta be good, and it's gotta be something that everybody can actually sing.

And I was like: Okay, I'm down.

And so I started playing a chord, and Mandy was like: Perfect.

And then she just lost her mind. LOL. We both did. Mandy and I just created like, one of the best songs I've ever heard, one of the best songs that's ever existed. It's simple, and beautiful, and the second you hear it, it's stuck in your head forever. We were firing on all cylinders, surfing right in the middle of the pipe, totally in the zone. If we really wanted to, we could probably get all the signatures we needed and all the votes and pass a law that replaces the old one and makes it official, but I think we both realized as we were singing it that we didn't really care if anyone else in the world ever heard it.

And I wanted to see how the song would sound if a normal person was singing it—like, I wanted to hear how it would sound if it weren't being done by these next-level, otherworldly pop megastars—and so I entered the void. I found old-man me just hanging around in the nothingness, and I taught him all the notes. And when I heard how it sounded coming out of his mouth, I almost cried, because it actually sounded *better*. It was actually like I wasn't even able to do the song justice with my voice as it is now. I had written the song for *him*.

And I guess Mandy must've been doing the same thing, because pretty soon, I could hear Future Mandy in there too. She showed up with her gray hair and her professor clothes, and she sounded just like Mandy, but her voice was so much richer, so much deeper, so much more full of life.

And pretty soon, Mandy herself showed up, and it was the four of us in the void: me, and Mandy, and Future Mandy the professor, and Future me the naked, saggy, tatted old man. And we were all just singing our hearts out, four normal people who didn't exist.

The funny thing about a book like this is that by the time you're reading it, you'll probably already know more about my life than I do. Just because I stop writing, that doesn't mean the gears stop turning. I'll still be me. You can still count on the fact that whenever I do anything, *someone* is gonna write about it *somewhere*. Once, I was arrested in Idaho for having weed on my tour bus, and the news was playing on the TV in the police station, and they interrupted this really serious reporter—she was talking about a protest in Pittsburgh over this black guy who got shot by the cops—and they cut her off mid-sentence and said: We're sorry, but we have to report on some breaking news. And they cut to a picture of the mugshot I had just taken half an hour ago and started describing the details of my arrest. So I'm not really worried about leaving anything out. If you're curious about something, you can bet that somebody else will cover it. In a way, it's easier to know everything about my life than it is to know nothing.

Maybe by the time you're reading this, the second season of *The Winstocks* will have already premiered. Or maybe you'll know what Mandy ended up majoring in in college. Or maybe you'll know what ended up happening to Oddvar and the seed vault. Or maybe I'll already be dead or in rehab or living off in the mountains somewhere. I don't know.

Something I've been thinking about a lot is what it would be like to read this book if you'd never heard of me before. I mean, obviously, most people who pick it up are gonna be fans of me or at least *interested* in my story, but I've been fantasizing about someone coming across it sometime way in the future, or someone just picking it up randomly at the library or in the airport when they're in a hurry and wanting something to read. I keep asking myself what it would be like to approach my life totally fresh like that, you know? If the entirety of my being were contained in these pages.

How would *that* person want the book to end?

What would they be curious about?

I guess I almost wish that person would think this was a piece of fiction—like, I guess I almost wish they'd think someone made me up—because then they could imagine whatever they wanted about me for the rest of their lives. They'd be relieved of the burden of caring about what happens to me, relieved of the stress of keeping tabs.

Sometimes, I just walk around my house or I'm just

eating dinner, and I can feel all this stress coming in from all these people I've never met, all these people I don't know. It's like I can feel it seeping in through the walls—these people grinding their teeth and holding their breath because they can sense that it's not gonna turn out well for me. Their whole body is telling them that, whether they like it or not, they're a part of this story, and there's no way it has a happy ending.

And for a lot of them, I think that makes them resent me, you know, because they never asked for this. I never asked if I could come into their lives, and they never asked for the responsibility. I just sort of opened the door one day and said: Hi! I'm here now. And a lot of them have their own methods of coping: Like, a lot of them are already sort of ironically predicting my downfall, and a lot of them are being really intense all the time about how meaningless I am and how little I matter to them, and a lot of them are sort of hedging their bets with as many people like me as possible so that whenever one of us falls or disappoints them or goes crazy in some predictable way, they can be like: That's okay. I've got so many of these guys in my cupboard that I don't have to mourn the loss of one of them for more than a second. And even the ones who love me, you know, like even the ones who've "chosen" to make me a part of their lives, even they sometimes feel like people who are just trying to make sense of this intrusion, just trying to take ownership over the trauma.

And I guess all I'd like to say to everybody is I'm sorry. I'm sorry you never really asked for me. I'm sorry I forced my way in. I know you're just trying to live your own life without having to live mine too.

When I started all this, I would tell myself that I was just a kid trying hard to reach out to people, just a guy from St. James trying to touch the whole world. And, in a way, that's true, but it doesn't change the fact that I *knew*. I always knew what I was doing. Even when I was just starting out with my dad, I knew that we were trying to pull off an *invasion*. We wanted to muscle our way into the bloodstream, sneak ourselves into the soil, infect as many bodies as we could. And we didn't really care about the violence, we weren't going to stop until the mission was complete.

And now here we are. Here I am living inside you. And I hope you can forgive me.

Maybe it'd be really healthy for everybody to just think of me as a character for a while. Even if you know it's a lie, even if the illusion will be broken in a week or a day or a minute, maybe it'd be really good to imagine that I'm no bigger or smaller than anything else you'd ever read in a book.

Maybe then you could close the cover on me and put me away on your shelf.

Maybe then you could move on to the next story.

Maybe then we could all be free.

The day that Mandy and I created our new national anthem, we didn't end up kissing or anything.

We actually just ended up watching all our old videos online—we kind of fell into this internet hole where we kept pulling up different music videos and live performances that we'd done over the years. We went through

Be My Baby and *Heartache/Heartbreak* and *Roses and Mud* and *Mobilize*, and every video we watched, we just found it so hilarious. We were teasing each other every time one of us would do a stupid dance move, and we were losing our shit at all the outfits we used to wear, and after a while, everybody else from the barbecue started wondering where we were and came to look for us, and they found us down in my studio watching all that shit, and pretty soon, we were all gathered around watching the videos, and it was like we were flipping through a family photo album or something, you know? It was actually really nice.

Later that night, after everyone went home, I ended up going online and posting all those tracks I made with my dad way back in the day—all those covers we recorded at the radio station in St. James. I didn't have the rights or anything, so I just threw them all up on my website for free. I didn't even think twice about it. I even included that crazy cover my dad sent me a few days before he killed himself.

And now everybody's talking about it like that's the fourth album, and it's like: Why not, you know? It might as well be.

I haven't given it a name yet or anything, but I guess once I do, I'll have to update the tat on my arm with all the album titles.

The next morning, I went out and got a different tattoo.

I called up Optimus, and I was like: Yo, I know it's a holiday, but do you think you could fit me in for a session? And he was like: Yeah, bro, I got you, drop by the spot.

And so I went to the parlor, and I had Optimus do a little something on my heart right under the seagull. I took a picture of it and emailed it to the graphic designer already so she could update the diagram, but she hasn't given it a number yet.

For now, I'll just describe it for you:

It's a little shotgun going off with the shell flying out of it. And on the shell, in really tiny letters, it says:

"Happy Fourth of July, everybody. Stay safe."

LOL.

ACKNOWLEDGMENTS

Thank you to Caroline Zancan, my brilliant editor.

Thank you to Henry Dunow, my agent and friend.

Thank you to Amy Glickman, Eli Gottlieb, and Kerry Cullen, my champions.

Thank you to Beth Heffron and Richard Kuritzkes, my always supportive parents.

Thank you to Jonathan Gordon, Isabel Siskin, Will Epstein, Mark Epstein, David Klass, Sander Gusinow, Sean Patrick McGowan, and Max Grey, my treasured early readers.

Thank you to Dianne McGunigle, my manager and confidant.

Thank you to Nicolas Jaar, my brother.

Thank you to Winnie Song, my eyes, ears, and conscience.

And thank you, finally, to Celine, my love. When I say I couldn't have written this book without her, I mean it quite literally. This book is dedicated to her, but that doesn't begin to cover it. I owe her everything and more, and it still won't be enough.

ABOUT THE AUTHOR

JUSTIN KURITZKES was born in Los Angeles and lives in New York. Productions of his plays have been staged by The New Group, JACK, and Actors Theatre of Louisville. He is known on the internet for his "Potion Seller" video and for his pop album, *Songs About My Wife*. He has been awarded residencies from Yaddo, the MacDowell Colony, and the Edward F. Albee Foundation. This is his first novel.